i-o

i-o

a collection of short stories

Published by:

prime
P.O. Box 36503, Canton, OH 44735, USA
www.primebooks.net

For more information, contact **prime**.

ISBN: 1-894815-05-X

i-o

simon logan

prime
P.O. Box 36503, Canton, OH 44735, USA
www.primebooks.net

contents

prism:
the mechanisation and deconstruction of beauty

In my workshop I had found a reflection of her. A construction of glass shards, breakages, fragments. There were headlights, windshields, watch faces, various degenerative pieces. Together they had come, a multitude collision of glass, to form a figure such as I had never seen before. For though she was composed almost entirely of edges, like a great diamond, she was utterly smooth—not ragged like the rest of us.

She had been encased in a great steel mess, a crumpled ball of metal of which I was charged the duty of breaking down.

That is what we do here—me and the other engineers.

Because of the way we had been born, limbs and faces augmented with razor-edges and tiny mechanisms for grinding and scoring, it was left for us to reconstitute the old metal so that it could make way for the new metal. An endless stream of garbage which we would process with our teeth and claws and leave for the immense trucks, almost tanks, to collect and take to the next stage in the production line.

Because of the way we had been born.

And because of the way I had been born, a slight flaw in Nature's own production line, I existed with a rusted oxygen tank stapled to my back, the wires that coiled my degraded body feeding me the purified chemical which my body could not find for itself. A thick black tube rose from the top of the tank, split into two smaller tubes; one embedded in the back of my neck, the other leading to a plastic mask that sat over my mouth and nose. The mask was yellowed by time and the dozens of noxious chemicals that floated around me so that my air constantly tasted of battery acid.

My special little deformation meant that I worked alone, in a corrugated steel shack at the back of the wrecking yard and away from the others. It meant I listened distantly to their shouts, the sound of their machines. It meant I never truly slept for my breathing apparatus wouldn't let me lie down properly. And it meant that I was content, because at least my deformities inside were given external form and kept others away; most of the time.

So when I found her in amongst a sprawl of bundled iron, steel and wire mesh I had the luxury of freeing her, like a gem embedded in a lump of coal, without anyone else knowing about her. She had no features to speak of but instead was described by that which was around her—a reflection of all the grime and waste metal that made them somehow beautiful. She was smeared with engine oil and milky-grey grease which I soon set about wiping off of her.

I could not believe how much she sparkled. I had seen nothing like her.

The rising siren that indicated the end of a shift sounded, resonating off of every piece of scrap in the yard. I hurriedly covered her with a piece of canvass, looping the hooks set into the concrete flooring through the holes in the sheet, securing her protection.

Then I prepared myself.

I went to the front window of the shack and noticed that already the others had begun to eagerly gather, emerging from amidst the wrecked automobiles piled high atop each other, from manhole covers that led into the bowels of the wrecking yard, where workers emerged like jagged phoenix, skin singed black by the heat of the furnaces down there, and from high, high above, clambering down from the makeshift ladders that rose as far into the air as was possible to see.

The joint between my mask and the tubing that led to it began to click with effort as my speeding pulse asked for more oxygen. The wires that came out of the tank tingled against me.

Perhaps twenty-five in all swarmed on the open area before my shack, each subtly different from the next but each very much the same. Variations on a theme; flaws in the production line.

Some removed pieces of clothing, stripping to the scarred, metal-laced flesh that lay beneath. Other spread motor oil over themselves as they laughed with each other. They were warming up.

I saw three of them begin to come towards me, the same as always, to try and entice me into their battles. I think they imagined it would be interesting to see how the cripple would fare in one of their brawls. No doubt bets were being placed on whether I would come out that night or not. There must still be a few that were willing to take the chance that I would, after all this time, finally agree—if not purely because of the winnings they would surely receive on such a ludicrous bet.

I was suddenly aware of the great shape behind me, swathed in the canvas sheet, glittering beneath it and perhaps even through it. I glanced back, panicking.

They must not find her.

So before they could reach my shack I began to undo the chains that locked me in here (and them out there). I opened the door when they were a mere three paces away, much to their surprise.

A ripple ran through the others at this alteration in the nightly ritual. Usually they would taunt me through the heavy aluminium door or one of the shack's grimy windows. It was rare enough that I should leave my shack at all, never mind when there were so many of them gathered around me.

I peered out of the gap I had allowed in the doorway, stopping the three in their tracks.

For a moment, all was silence, save for the muffled, distant sounds of other workyards and the great engines that powered them. The workers stared at me, at my face so distorted by my mask.

One of the three looked back at his fellows questioningly.

I had begun to regret the move, for instead of preventing them from getting close enough to the creature I had found to discover her, I had instead ignited a curiosity in them as to why I was not doing as I always did. Creatures of the production line were we all—our lives a constant, unending, repetition. It was how we existed.

This was not repetition.

"Will you be joining us tonight?" the worker at the forefront of the trio asked, returning to the interaction's template. He was bare across a set of muscled shoulders, both hands ending in fleshy pincers lined with tiny metal teeth. He stood with his legs far apart, his booted feet embedded in the soft dust of the scrapyard's ground.

My breathing apparatus hissed steam from a pneumatic vent in its side.

I shook my head.

Another few moments of silence followed, then laughter from somewhere way back—an infection that quickly spread until they were all laughing. At me. The coward who would not fight—and in relief that the pattern had returned.

The one who had spoken to me bowed his head regally, exposing the plating that capped his skull, perhaps as a result of a previous night's entertainment.

I tried to hold their gaze but, as usual, could not and found myself staring at the ground. I watched, out of the corner of my eye, until the three returned to the rest and then there were shouts and on the first clash of metal on metal I retreated back into the shack.

I collapsed once inside, my breathing tank hissing angrily at my exertion, weighing me onto the cold floor and the closest creature to sleep that I would encounter visited upon me—unconsciousness.

I emerged some time later. There is little difference between night and day in this part of the city—the thick black smoke we churn out hanging so heavily above us that it becomes like a parent's smothering embrace—so the only way we have to measure the passage of time is by each other's activities.

Although most will descend on the lot for the daily fights, the maintenance workers are the first to return to work for they must care for the machines in the short times between shifts. The others retreat to their quarters to rest before the routine, like a snake chasing its own tail, comes full circle and they are working again.

I do not sleep and spend most of the time looking out the shack's sole window at the strange patterns that the smoke funnels paint upon the sky. There are no stars to gaze upon. Just the great, riveted, black heaven.

But before peering out of my window that night I first checked Prism, as my unconscious mind's meanderings decided to call her, as it was to the immense, swollen fear that she should be gone that I woke. I touched the tarpaulin sheet covering her and half-expected it to tumble beneath my touch.

My hydraulic lungs hissed with relief when I felt her beneath.

I peeled the sheet away in one corner, around a protuberance that could have been a human breast. I watched, spellbound as she sparkled at me, as if she were speaking to me in each flicker and twist of light. A thousand faces were in that shape, reflecting the grime around me without repeating it, somehow reinventing a cleaner, purer world. And in one, my face, not disjointed or broken up by my breathing apparatus but like the others; better still. I moved my jaw; the reflection moved it's.

I felt the urge to lean forward and press my lips to her when another reflection caught my eye. I turned suddenly, just missing the rapid movement in the shack's window. Hurriedly, I pulled the sheet back across her and pulled an old machine that had once been used for stamping coins in front of her for extra protection.

I peered through the pane and glimpsed a number of the other engineers roaming amongst the trash, gnawing on rusted iron plating and coils of barbed wire. I could sense their desire to look back at me, could see in the way they fought so hard *not* to look in my direction that they had a reason not to do so. They moved like insects.

I could almost taste their curiosity. They knew I had something.

They would never get her.

This continued for days.

With each moment I ached to look at her once more, to reassure myself that I had really found her but as time passed I grew more afraid of doing so, for in their impatience the others had begun to encroach upon my shack. More than once I caught one of them staring in through the window and it became harder and harder to prevent them coming too close when the time came for the fights. I noticed in their offer, now, a distraction that betrayed their greater interest in another topic.

What it was that had been causing me to act so strangely.

One night they managed to lure me further through the
door than I would have liked, confusing me, and a serpen-
tine creature who cleaned the chimney shafts almost
slipped behind me and inside. I slammed the door on it,
catching a fold of it's scaly flesh before it pulled loose then
was treated to wave of shouts and things being thrown at
the shack's walls.

Soon after I placed a sheet of steel across the window,
nailgunning it into place, shutting them all out.

I didn't answer the next night when they tapped on my
door.

Nor the next.

I hid inside in that time, continuing my work as normal
during my shift, then listening to their brawls at night. The
collision of metal, their grunts and cries of pain. Things
snapping, shredding. The silence that beckoned afterwards. While they battled I caressed Prism beneath her
ugly shawl and as the days progressed I found myself sliding underneath the sheet and joining her in the oily darkness.

She taught me beauty I had never known. In her manifold faces she reflected every possibility, every variation.
Species of population, each as unique are the next. Places
beyond the sky. She told me of the wonder of things.

And in return I would polish her, clean her. I would ca-
ress her as a lover and began to learn her shape as if it were
a memory. I taught myself her contours; she revealed me to
myself.

How she glistened for me.

Then the nights came when their battles seemed to de-
tach from the dusty arena outside and refocus on my shack
itself. They rained against the thin metal walls, shouting
and calling, running hooked fingers down the corrugation.
The roofing lurched with their weight as they scrambled
upon it. They gnawed at the plating I had placed across the
window.

And still I fled to Prism's infinite shine. Defiantly, I had
begun removing her shawl for small periods at a time, letting her illuminate the shack and dilute some of the filth
that pervaded it. Perhaps I expected her to repel them or
even transform them as they were transformed upon her
multitude surfaces. She did neither.

I felt like we were protecting each other.

But the days were dwindling before me as if viewed myopically. I began tasting the flakes of scrap metal in my air as the tanks neared drying up and knew that soon they would have to be replaced. The others must have known this too for like everything else, my tanks were renewed in adherence to a strict schedule and they abruptly became quiet at night. Instead they would stalk the shack predatorily, their shuffling footsteps and muffled whispers the only sounds I could hear.

And while we both waited for the next shift, which would signal the replacement of my tanks, I kissed Prism on every one of her shining surfaces.

I had considered the moment during the many shifts leading up to it.

I stood behind the shack's door, disfigured hands pressed softly against its cold surface and listened to the conspicuous silence outside. I had replaced Prism's covering and moved more objects around her though in the end it would make no difference. The shack was ten feet by ten feet; there was little room to hide *anything*.

I undid the locks then waited a moment before opening the door a crack. It was relatively bright outside, a false light from the harsh floodlights littering the city reflecting off the low cloud cover, and dust from the ground blew in miniature storms. I peered as far as my line of sight would allow but there was no sign of the new tanks.

Already my lungs ached, my head swollen with blood loss, tingling. My whole body was weak and inefficient.

I opened the door further and at the same time I saw the new tank lying upon the hard-baked ground. I saw the first of them, squatting by a pile of girders, hands hanging in his lap. The tank was in the dead centre of their bloody arena. I could see pieces of them left over from previous battles scattered around my new lungs, lying on one side behind drag marks that revealed where they had pulled it further away from me.

I wondered whether I would be able to make it that far.

I wondered whether it would be worth it.

Perhaps I could die in there, reflected in Prism. Perhaps I would not die as long *as* she reflected me. Perhaps *nothing* died as long as she reflected it.

There was more movement and I saw others amidst the rubble, glints of light where welding goggles shone.

They had been preparing for this moment just as I had.

They began to crawl into the opening slowly, arachnids of metallic texture, waiting to see what I would do. Some glanced into the dark crack the door's opening allowed in an early attempt to discover what I had been concealing from them.

They would never know just how dangerous, how perfect Prism was.

But there was so much more to learn from her. I was sure she could reflect so much more to me if I were given the time. I may even have been able to figure a way to bring her out of the shack so that she might be able to reflect more and more. It could not end here.

So I closed the door of my shack behind me and for the first time in weeks was out in the open air. My skin crawled and my lungs bucked at the ugly air. I coughed into the plastic moulded mask and felt my body's urge to collapse but remained standing. Cautiously, I took my first step, a hundred eyes upon me.

They began to move in response, the way they crouched making them look like a cricket's athletic back legs about to spring them towards me, towards the shack, towards the interminable beauty inside.

I continued towards the tank, my eyes flitting from it to the debris around me and those who lay within it. I could sense them swarming behind me but knew they had not reached the shack yet. As I drew closer, I felt so terribly exposed at my rear and instinctively turned.

Dry, callous steam erupted from my breathing pack, the few last gasps it could manage. My leg shuddered, then collapsed under me and I fell to the ground. There was a sudden rush of movement that quickly halted when I managed to get to my knees. They lurked at the edge of my vision, their deformities clicking and snapping rhythmically. They were like carrion vultures around me.

I wasn't going to make it.

I began to turn and all I could think of was Prism, alone and exposed, but they were already moving in on me and so I scrambled forwards on hands and knees towards the tank, thinking that if I could just reach that and get it connected quickly enough I would be able to make it back before they would reach her.

The dust and grit swirled around me and I began gasping for oxygen and as I clawed my way forwards I realised I should have done more for her, shouldn't have just waited there. I could have tunnelled my way through the soft ground beneath the shack and helped her escape. *Something.*

I was fully extended, my legs towards the shack, my arms towards the tank, as if I were wading into a stream whose current I feared; too far in and I would be swept away. And then my hand was on the tank and hope felt all that more real. The others continued to close in around me, still too unsure to make a move into the shack yet, though several were close enough to do so.

I snapped the plug out of the tank I wore with my withered, shaking hands, and quickly struggled with the new one. The connection was made, the fittings clicking into place. I awaited the lighting stench of the first breath of the fresh, undiluted oxygen that would carry me back to Prism but instead was filled with a putrid, searing energy that stung my every pore and too late I realised the bastards has poisoned the tank.

It was the sound of a great turbine that aroused me and as I came too I spat globules of red- and black-tinged saliva onto the ground. My whole body felt as it if were filled with acid, as if the stuff flowed through my veins and watered my head, soaked my brain. I realised through the haze that my breathing apparatus had been taken from me, that I now breathed the polluted air that my body so rejected at the same time I realised that the only turbine that made a sound that loud was that which drove the crushing machine.

Tears bled involuntarily from me as arms reached under me and rolled me over onto my back. The other engineers loomed over me and I could see the hatred, the jealously in their eyes. Above me, the great pneumatic crane that operated in conjunction with the crusher dazzled me with a brightness that was not its own; that could be no other.

Behind me, the sounds of my shack being destroyed.

And so, as I whimpered silently in pain and the anger of one who is utterly helpless, they made me watch as Prism was slowly, slowly lowered into the crushing machine.

Out of mass-production she came and into it she returned.

I listened to her being torn into shards, hating how much her breakage sounded like a great, unending scream.

Only at the belly of night (what we call night) do I emerge from the pit which I now work in, when the toxins are thinner. There is a hatch in its roof that lets me out into the world, no window. They built it for me, afterwards, from the broken pieces of my shack.

They do not bother me any more, the others. I'm not sure why.

Maybe they realise that they have committed an act more vile than they understand it to be. Maybe they too hear her screams still, in the glow of the floodlights.

My body has just about recovered from the trauma of that night. My mind has not been so lucky.

I can feel the scars on the inside of my lungs when I breathe now. I can feel what they did to me; and her.

And so, unfettered, I wander the yard, which goes on for miles, in the belly of the night.

I look for her in the trash, the rubble, the debris. I look for her in car headlights. In windscreens. In pieces of broken glass and bottles. In chrome plates and hub caps.

I stare into a hundred empty, monochrome reflections each night.

They have recycled her, re-mixed her. She is now a different version of herself.

But they cannot destroy her completely.

She is in there, somewhere. She pervades the monotony, the endless stream of products we deliver to the trucks that collect our work. I take pride in the knowledge that she may be teaching many thousands of others rather than just me.

I miss her, though.

And I will find her again, if she does not find me first.

PIRAEUS 3/99

coaxial

creature

[above]

coaxial-creature [above]

I live with the sound of static in my ears, up here amongst the pylons.

The network of transmission stations, communications cabling and electrical supply lines has grown above the city far below like some great mechanical spider's coaxial web. Which would make me, and the other engineers, the flies trapped within.

It was getting nearer the next electrical surge (they were set to a schedule laid out by an atomic clock but most of us still relied on our own senses to know when one was due) so we had begun to finish up our work and move towards the nearest rubber station.

There was a latent electrical charge in the cables at all times which our suits and gloves protected us from for the most part. But when a surge came, a tidal wave of hundreds of thousands of volts that exploded along the power lines in one sudden, raging blast we had to climb inside one of the man-sized vulcanised balls that were scattered around between the pylons and towers, a cocoon of sour-smelling latex—the rubber stations.

The cabling network ran for tens of miles in every direction, wafer thin wire and foot-wide pipes, spiralling twists of plastic-coated filaments, metal struts to support them and to link communications towers. Hundreds of [and at times a thousand] feet below lay Reykjavik, nothing more than a mass of concrete obscenities, high-rises, sky-scrapers scabbed with dirt and plague and the solid black veins of traffic that ran between them. We were high enough up in the steel-grey sky that a gossamer layer of cloud was there for us to reach out and touch if we so wished.

I crawled along a tentacle of metallic tubing, the heavy chains which hung from my work belt wrapped around it. This was merely a precautionary measure; we pylon engineers only very rarely fell or lost our balance. Across the vast cabling system the others were crawling into their vulcanised wombs for a few moments rest.

I finally reached a rubber station, nestled in the crook of a transmission tower about eight hundred feet up, and peeled back the opening as if it were a wound, unclipping my chains and crawling inside.

It was only there, in the glowing red stomach, that we realised how noisy it was amidst the pylons. The high-altitude winds that scoured and scraped the metal, the drone of electricity and the mindless white noise of endless static—they all seemed to fade with familiarity until we didn't even realise they were there. Until, of course, we were met with the muffled silence of the rubber stations.

There was less than a minute to the surge.

Often, I would find remnants of previous occupants inside the great balls—leftover pieces of food, water bottles, a damaged tool or a small bag of circuitry—but this time it was empty. A small black and white television screen, like the thousands that were mounted on the broadcast lines for some unknown reason, glowed softly in one corner.

I removed my backpack and unzipped the main compartment.

Thirty seconds to the surge.

Everyone would be inside by now, wherever they were. Somehow we always managed to make it to an empty rubber station and would never have to share with another worker—at least it had never happened to me in the seven years since I had left Lo-Fi. There was a strange, twisted bond between us, one that was formed by the mere fact we were up here together and therefore did not need any actual interaction to make it tangible or to reinforce it.

From my backpack I removed a device I had begun constructing myself some months earlier. It had taken me time to scavenge all the necessary pieces from the irregular clots of mechanical refuse that you could find up here so I had only just finished work on it in the previous few weeks. It was the result of a curiosity that had been with me ever since I had started work amongst the pylons and one which I knew at least feather-touched the other workers from time to time -

To look out across the cables and piping as a surge ran through it all—to see this Hi-Fi world through the bright blue veil of twelve-hundred-thousand volts of electricity.

It was not possible for us to even safely peek out from the opening in the rubber stations because any crack in the vulcanised shell would let the horrendous and wild energies come charging in. I had only once seen the result of someone who had tried to bear witness—several of us had converged upon the black and charred husk of the man's lower body wedged in the gap of his rubber station, his upper torso having crumbled and dropped towards Lo-Fi, towards the city far below.

This is why the device I had constructed was based around a pair of soldering goggles which, when worn, would allow me to see, to a limited degree, through the thick red skin of the rubber station. I had built a series of mirror and UV mechanisms into the eyepieces, with a solid mass of broken circuitry held in place on one side by tattered electrical tape. It was a crude, uncomfortable invention, one that fucked up my vision for an hour or so after I'd been wearing them but was worth it—to see the faces of gods and viruses assembled together in the static and white lightning that the others were numb and blind to.

Ten seconds left and I strapped the goggles onto my head. They sat awkwardly on one side so I had to hold them steady as I pressed my face to the red skein. My pulse counted the beats to the surge, little waves of blood in my veins, a tribal drumbeat.

And the energies came like a great volcanic flow of perfect blue-white, smooth and jagged and rampaging as it seared the cables, the machinery, poured over the rubber bubbles we hid in, shook them, and cracked the sky in two for split seconds at a time. I watched it all unfold before me through a hazed and muddy viewpoint, absently aware of its beauty, and thought how wonderful it was that the static had saved me just when I was doubting my decision to leave Lo-Fi.

In the illumination I saw the outlines of the other engineers huddled in their bubbles, I saw cities hundreds of miles away, I saw the glitter of static made real like great

clouds of silver aluminium confetti. And then, in the
surge's twilight, I saw something scuttling along a thick,
reinforced shaft a few hundred metres away. It shone in
the electrical buzz and I got the impression of multiple
limbs before everything went silent and black once more.

I stayed where I was, momentarily blinded and unable
to move. The afterimage of what I'd seen was burned on
my retinas and I felt that if I moved even that would vanish. I turned the impression over and over in an attempt to
understand it.

After a few seconds, that purple reflection faded too and
I slumped to the floor, fumbling to decipher what I had just
seen.

[lo-fi]

The base-world; ground level Reykjavik. Where there is
a solid pavement on a solid piece of land. Where the buildings rise from, where many of the pylons and towers have
their pneumatic roots. Where the air is thick and
smog-bound and filled with chemicals. Where people
walk and crowd together like a black, gelatinous mass.
Where you are stripped of all feelings and forced to face
the cold, hard shell of alienation. Where there is poison
and sexual fluids and shallow graves.

[hi-fi]

Amongst the pylons, the cables, the circuitry. Where TV
stations blast out their broadcasts in shuddering waves
that can be seen in the air itself when the lighting is right.
Where there are no gentle breezes, only aggressive winds.
Where broadbands carry digital harmonies and there is
devastating coldness. Where you are allowed to escape the
rigours of humanity and left to find your own level of existence.

On a night when the sky was so filled with dense grey
clouds that it seemed to be a patchwork dome of concrete
hemming the world in I saw the coaxial-creature again.

It had been four nights and in that time I had moved towards the outskirts of the cabling network where the wires
became thinner and the TV screens' pictures more grainy.
There was a re-run of an old American game show on, any
sound that would normally accompany it drowned out by
the hiss of wind and the sparks I ignited with my blow-

torch. The hosts' jacket seemed to trouble the small black and white screen, a confusion of too many non-colours.

I watched the game show distantly as I repaired a break in the cabling. The next surge was growing slowly closer, a scent like burnt tires filling the air. I thought about what we had found that night previously—the shredded rubber zones and the body impaled on a small outward-facing satellite—and considered again my decision not to say anything to the others.

I hadn't known what I had seen—that was what I had told myself.

My vision has been damaged by the goggles—that was what I now supposed.

The crackle of static seemed to fade around me all of a sudden, leaving a cold desert wind to whisper amongst the metal. I shut off my blowtorch and fought the urge to look over my shoulder.

Steel girders creaked under their own weight. A piston fired lazily.

I almost felt a movement. I almost looked.

But then the feeling was gone. Static crackled. For a moment, I heard the voice of the game show host and drone of a buzzer. Balloons fell onto the woman on the screen as she jumped up and down. The game show host smiled at the camera as his jacket danced in a crazy mesh of colours around him.

Half an hour later I was inside a rubber zone. Everyone had been getting into them faster lately. I'd even seen an argument break out the night before as two workers rushed for the same shelter.

I huddled in one corner as I snacked on some rice bread. The goggles lay temptingly on top of my knapsack and I couldn't help but look at them as I ate.

The bubble suddenly began to shudder as the energies started, a deafening roar searing my ears. Lightning cracked whip-like against the red-orange skein, this time feeling a little more dangerous than it usually did; a little more predatory.

I had stopped chewing when the electrical storm had started. When that happens, you stop everything subconsciously. It holds you, demanding every moment of your attention.

And yet still I managed to reach for the goggles, doing so without any thought process being present to enable me to do so. I just did. I fumbled numbly to get them on, knowing that the barrage would end soon and that I might miss my chance to . . . to what?

I fixed the strap around my head, hesitated a few inches from the bubble's interior. I had seen nothing since that night. Nobody else had gone missing as far as we were aware but there were hundreds of us here and we didn't know one any more than we knew the next. How would we know if anyone else went missing unless there was a body as before? How could *I* know that many hadn't *already* been taken, unnoticed?

I pressed my face to the rubber and flicked a switch on the side of the goggles, initiating the slight hum it gave off. The lenses re-mixed the world outside to a new palette of colours and shapes, a hyper-ballad of sensual input that dizzied me upon first glance and got worse the longer I looked.

I saw bright red gashes of ball lighting floating through the pylons like wandering suns, sparks showering from support lines. The sky was lit from behind like a Chinese puppet show in a purple the colour of blood in a fresh corpse's veins and the puppets were giant steel meshworks, great struts and girders and interlocking cables, a forest of deadly metal constructs and then a shape too, a spidery skittering shape thirty feet across glimpsed in strobe-light for milliseconds at a time—scurrying across a nearby broadband power wire, moving without touching anything, leaping from pylon to pylon and then pausing, turning—gone.

I started breathing again about a minute after the currents had faded to nothing.

Another two bodies were discovered and something began to happen.

We who supposedly knew no fear for we lived hundreds of feet above solid concrete amongst millions of volts of electrical energy were terrified.

I saw the others begin to congregate in small groups as they worked next to one another. Every absentee was noticed and became cause for concern, whereas before they would simply be assumed to have moved further afield, if noticed at all. There began a re-thinking of past events, of those who had vanished [thought to have gone back to Lo-Fi] and those who had perished [apparently while trying to glimpse the storm].

How long has it been amongst us? they asked. What does it want?

I still hadn't told anyone about what I had seen, what I knew was out there. I kept my distance from the rest, especially when they gathered to discuss the matter, making sure my work details took longer than necessary.

They didn't even know what *it* was, like I did.

They thought is was the storms becoming worse or some electronic god-virus set to drive us mad. They had never glimpsed that great, multi-limbed creature that shone and sparkled as it moved so quickly and so gracefully through the cable-sky like an giant squid emerging from the black depths of the ocean.

I, however, saw it wherever I looked.

Part imagination, part damaged retina, the creature seemed to be formed of every random arrangement of cables and poles that I laid my eyes upon. It was the side of a transmission pylon with three thick wires snaking around it for limbs and a neatly placed girder stick out towards me. It was curled up in a nest of dead cables discarded by other workers on a platform high up in the complex. It was the shadow-thing that was always at the corner of your eye.

It haunted me.

One night I dream of falling and I no longer know whether it is terror or exhilaration that coats me in the fine sweat I awaken to. Sinking to Lo-Fi like that, with metal flashing past me at three hundred miles an hour, I am like a butterfly being pounded by the rain, spiralling towards the traffic, the all-night gas stations, the glowing neon sign of Iceland's first McDonalds.

As I unclip myself from the struts I had secured myself to an hour earlier I notice how cautiously the others all move now, how they keep looking over their shoulders and how they glance in my direction—like they know.

It must have become noticeable over the weeks that I hadn't participated once in their huddled discussions about what was amongst them. Did they suspect I knew something? Or worse, did they suspect I had something to do with the continued deaths and disappearances?

Four workers had already returned to Lo-Fi, something almost unheard of amongst us while contracts were still active. They'd simply climbed back down, pylon by pylon, until they were the same specks of black that the others down there were.

Two nights ago I had been aware of a small group of them subtly converging on my workspace. I had climbed the tower I was on to its peak, unhurriedly so that they wouldn't think I was avoiding them, then crawled across some cabling that sagged under my weight, then pretended to resume my work there. They watched me for a time, discreetly, then moved on.

I did not know exactly what they would do if they got close to me but I became suddenly very protective of myself and my knapsack. I feared that they would find the goggles inside and somehow use them as evidence of my guilt and considered throwing them away but I couldn't. I had become enthralled by the site of the illuminated heavens; I obsessed about the creature I had seen stalking us.

Despite the risk, I kept the goggles.

But I had had to sleep. It had been two weeks since my last rest and I hadn't been able to delay it any longer. I had climbed as far as I could and decided I would settle for an hours sleep, enough to get me through another week—any more would risk them sneaking up on me.

As it was, it was later, when I was fully awake and in the middle of replacing a magnet in one of the TV screens that they somehow managed to get close to me. They were in a vague circle that made me think of a spider's web, a construction of crooked concentric circles drawing closer and closer—and that made me think of the creature.

I edged away but this time they followed me insistently, adjusting their approach. The air was unusually warm that night, swirling awkwardly around me, making my hands clammy beneath my gloves. More seemed to converge from above—I saw them when I looked up and froze where I was.

It all seemed so planned.

I looked down, through the steel latticework that made up our world and onto the tiny city far below etched in grey and black like the sad portrait of a manic depressive. A light rain had begun to fall, silver bullets that could be followed all the way to the concrete if you so wished.

My fears of falling to Lo-Fi swelled in my head, behind my damaged, reddened eyes. I blinked away the constant stream of tears that the goggles seemed to cause.

More of them now, drawing closer like a mob.

Would they throw me off if they suspected I was responsible? Of course they would.

I backed along the wide pipe I sat on, slipping on the rain-slicked surface.

I should tell them, I should tell them what I knew.

I didn't know if I'd ever get the chance; or that I'd take it if I did.

They all stopped suddenly when the foremost were less then thirty feel away from me. I felt more looming above me like insects. Some were sniffing the air. A bright, arm-sized crackled split the air to my left.

In my fear I had failed to notice that a surge was growing near.

For a time, the others didn't move, seeming caught between converging on me and the need to find safety in a rubber zone. Particularly with the rain it would be vital to get inside one as soon as possible because moisture had a tendency to conduct the electricity and encourage its earlier arrival.

Then one by one they began to retreat.

And I knew that next time I would not be so lucky.

Even inside the rubber zone I could tell the surge was going to be nastier than usual. The warm air, the rain—it was all conducive to the power of the surge.

I no longer even questioned whether to wear the goggles or not. They were on my face within moments of sealing the rubber skein, my eyes calmed by the inverse spectrum that they had become addicted to. My heart still pounded from the encounter moments before and I feared what might happen once the storm had passed.

They had seemed to have convinced themselves that I was a danger to them and yet despite this I could not imagine bringing myself to reveal my secret. I looked into a Technicolor Heaven every night—I couldn't let them take that away from me.

The electronic sirocco blew around my bubble, lightning gorging the air like a guillotine and behind it all was a low industrial drone that grew in power and volume with each passing moment as if it were detailing the countdown to the end of days. Despite the insistent rocking of the bubble I kept peering out into the ravaged sky, watching blue waves of energy pour along the cables and tubing, caressing them, teasing them.

And then the black shape of the coaxial-creature flashed across the horizon miles away, a flickering predator scuttling like a giant, wasted crab and it was coming for *me*. My breath caught in my throat as I fought to find it again, vanished amongst the shadows and metallic spinal cords of the communication towers.

There again, closer now and to the right, lingering over a rubber zone.

I glimpsed the shadow of the occupant flailing around inside.

Then gone, the rubber ball torn open and flapping spastically as the energies poured over it.

Then the image of the thing leaping downwards where the cables were thicker, out of my sight. I scrambled to the other side of my refuge, the goggles almost falling from my face and I had to hold them in place where the electrical tape had split.

Flash

Darkness

Flash

I struggled to make sense of the shapes spread out before me, everything merging into a mechanical spaghetti covered in bright red pustules.

Flash

I glimpsed it; I saw it.

Nearer. Back up high again, scrambling effortlessly across metal and mid-air.

Flash.

I had been watching this thing for weeks now, wondering if I were looking at the face of god or madness of both. It had been taking us one by one, throwing us back to Lo-Fi because we didn't belong up here, we were invaders.

I had been watching it –

And now it was watching me.

Flash.

Right above me.

A spider-black shape, cancer-thin limbs stretched out across my bubble, it's meaty fat body deposited on the rubber zone's apex.

The light held us, frozen.

In shadow, I could see parts of its head moving; it cocked its head to one side. The limbs became like tentacles, slithering around the rubber, embracing it.

I could hear it's breathing, low and steady. The surge was stopping.

I looked right into it's eyes.

The others would be emerging soon.

My eyes stung from the sights I had been privy to. I waited to be consumed as it continued to squeeze the bubble.

Then a flash of light and a scream that was the rubber exploding and there was hot, wet air all around me, the sudden force of it throwing me backwards and all I saw were eight ragged limbs flickering past me as I waited to be turned to dust by the surge but everything was quiet and smoking and the surge had just ended in time.

I was draped backwards across a rusted pipe, an eight-hundred foot drop below me on all sides. Rain and perspiration trickled down my face.

I looked into the face of the coaxial-creature and knew I was closer to death than I ever have been.

Its jaw muscles worked upon themselves, a bone protruding from either side of its face like dislocated arm joints, like pneumatic cylinders. What little skin it had crackled and sparked.

And then it launched it's head at me, mouth wide open and all I could do was throw myself backwards, off of the pipe—into the cold, empty, static air.

I remember the faces of some of the others as I fell past them, colliding occasionally with struts, crashing through a disused satellite, the coaxial-creature chasing me all the way until its limbs got caught up in the grated flooring of a platform I sailed by.

And I remember, the clear, fresh, pure feel of the air on my skin.

It's even more difficult now, living in Lo-Fi again.

As alien as the place had felt to me before I had gone Hi-Fi it was more so now. I'm still getting used to having solid ground beneath my feet.

I still wear all my chains. They hang uselessly from my waist when I walk around. I clip them to the ceiling of the warehouse I'm squatting in when I sleep so that I dangle ten feet above the air.

I move amongst the crowds, the commuters, mobile phones pressed to their ears, laptops clinging to their chests and it feels like I'm floating through them all. I know I don't belong there.

When I look up, the sky glitters and I know it is because it is full of a world of metal that used to be my home. And every once in a while I glimpse a shape skittering across it—a great, insectoid shape that is described only in shadow—and I understand again that I am safer down here.

I long to return to Hi-Fi—but I can't.

It rejected me, just as Lo-Fi rejected me and so I'm stuck in between.

I filled the warehouse with TV's to bring me the static buzz that was a constant up there. I sleep in mid-air for an hour once a fortnight. I spend most of my time trawling the city picking up electronic trash and fusing it together into semi-working models or sculptures.

One night I began to climb a pylon that led into the co-axial-network but I only got a hundred feet up before I stopped and turned back.

I still have the goggles.

And the face of a god is still burned into my eyes.

partofit

youarethemachineyouarethemachineyouarethemachine
youarethemachineyouarethemachineyouarethemachineyouarethem
youarethemachineyouarethemachineyouarethemachineyouarethem
youarethemachineyouarethemachineyouarethemachineyouarethem
youarethemachineyouarethemachineyouarethemachineyouarethem
youarethemachineyouarethemachineyouarethemachineyouarethem
youarethemachineyouarethemachineyouarethemachine

youarethemachineyouarethemachineyouarethemachineyouarethem
youarethemachineyouarethemachineyouarethemachineyouarethem
arethemachineyouarethemachine
youarethemachineyouarethemachineyouarethemachi
youarethemachineyouarethemachine
youarethemachineyouarethemachine
youarethemachineyouarethemachineyouarethemachine
youarethemachineyouarethemachineyouarethemachineyouaretha

you are not inside the machine
you are not a part of the machine
you are the machine
you   are   the machine
ou   are   the machi
machine

youarethemachineyouarethemachineyouarethem
youarethemachineyouarethemachineyouarethem
youarethemachineyouarethemachineyouarethem
youarethemachineyouarethemachineyouarethem
youarethemachineyouarethemachine

partofit

partofit

>I am an artist but
>I am a mechanik.
>I am a worker but
>I am a slave.
>I am dead pieces and yet
>I am alive.

>I am partofit.

I long ago realised that the cyclic pattern engraved into the metal conveyor belt endlessly passing before me was designed to lull. Like vicious words whispered softly, the ragged scratching became a gentle flow as long as it was moving. And it was always moving, for so was the production line.

The pattern has no effect if you look directly at it. It shudders through your vision, stabbing visual khaos between loads, when the parts stop coming momentarily. But beneath the conveyor's wet, meaty treasures the design comes alive. It gains a dark rhythm like a severed head's blood spurts, wraps itself around you with a feather touch and you are calmed. Held down for one more day.

And we don't even know its happening.

I too would have been like the rest if it had not been for the embolism some months ago.

>vacant wiry images, barbed wire feeding
>through my pulse, and then bleeding
>staccato shudders, a rejection of my own fluids
>as i fall coldly to the factory floor

>and left there for hours
>retrieved by a supervisor, clipboard
>pinned to his chest marks an 'X'
>next to my section allocation.

I have vague recollection of my recovery as the very tables and machines which my fellow workers operate were used to revive me. Metal pins in my legs and a series of hydraulic pistons placed by my temples to release the pressure when it is becoming too much.

A little alteration.

We all have them from time to time but I now ask myself which has changed me more—the rusted steel grafted to my face or that last vision as I fell to the spongy concrete floor, of something beyond a random etching in the belt's sheet metal.

A message.

The next part arrives before me and my examination of the pattern is interrupted.

A red, moist lump with several tube-like protrusions.

And, as I have done seventeen thousand eight hundred and seventy six times before, I reach into the pocket of my plastic bib, withdraw a small hollow pipe and peel back a layer of flesh from the part before me as if it were a mutated onion. I drive the pipe into the gap, then let the layer snap back into place.

I don't know what happens to the part in the next section, nor what processes it is subject to prior to mine. A patchwork of metal grows upward and outward on either side of me, blocking my view in every direction except the blank brick wall in front of me and the rusted and decaying staircase behind me. But I can hear the other workers. Though they are silent beneath the pneumatic hisses and raucous grinding of giant oil-slicked cogs turning a machine beyond our comprehension, I can hear them.

And they are screaming.

I watch the part, newly modified/upgraded/defaced, as it moves along the conveyor belt. It pauses before a gap in the ragged partition and I can see it twitch minutely.

Then is snatched up by a rusted claw-like device from beyond my workspace, jagged pincers clamping it firmly, squeezing ugly juices out, and the part is gone.

Once again the pattern on the conveyor belt is free of interference and I stare blankly at it's workings.

I lean forward as a slight rattling begins behind my eyes and I feel my blood soaring within me. I am aware of the tiny hydraulic pumps nestled in my temples beginning to work themselves; groaning, reluctant movements.

The etching slides before me and I am more certain than ever than it speaks glyphs.

I touch the pattern, let my scarred, emaciated fingers trace it's wyrd angles and hypnotic revolutions and something begins to reveal itself to me.

Steam suddenly pours from the chute to my left and even though the delivery of the parts is timed as precisely as every other piece of the machinery that engulfs me it surprises me.

I snatch my fingers back from the pattern and reach out to take the next part, my other hand already withdrawing another pipe from the stained and torn pouch upon my apron. But there is nothing within the steam.

I move my hand around for the part, ready for it's warm, wet feel, but as the cloud dissipates I see there is nothing there.

The clock has missed a beat; the wheel, a cog.

I reach out again to where the part should be, to where the parts always are and always will be, because this is all I know how to do. This is what I do.

But there is only blank, blank space there.

I wipe sweat from my brow and turn to the set of thin metal steps that lead upwards behind me to my resting quarters. The machine parts visible through the thin skein of the wall on either side move as they always have. I appeal to their repetitive nature, to ask them, my employers, my masters, what I should do.

They do not answer.

I turn back to the conveyor belt and see the pattern is not as random as before.

I reach out for the part that should be there and lift away hot, damp air.

The pounding in my head is growing again. The pistons grate angrily against my skull.

Then steam pours from the chute exactly when it should and I hear the thud of the next part's delivery.

Without thought, because this is how we are taught, I pick up the part, take a pipe from my pouch, peel back the layer, and insert it.

For a moment I pause and examine the part and it is exactly like each one before it, exactly like each one to come. And yet it is neither of these things.

I place it back on the conveyor belt an instant later and watch the claw device reach through and remove it.

The rhythm has returned.

And yet even now I can feel what lurked in that empty space where the missed part should have been. Fear. Panic. Disorder. The supervisors rushing around maniacally to soothe the machine, to recover its heartbeat.

It is only later that I will realise that this is what is written in the conveyor metal.

My sleep, as rhythmic as the swelling drones of the factory that constructed my world, was interrupted by an alien sound—alien for it was not created by machine, nor steel, nor suffering.

I opened my eyes without moving my head and watched the pieces that moved in the walls turning, grinding, maintaining the production line's heartbeat. Beneath the crackle of two cogs meeting I heard the sound that had awoken me. Soft, wet—organic.

My lips pursed involuntarily and I thought of burst pneumatic pipes leaking oils. I thought of mould dripping greenish condensation onto the concrete floors like poison milk from a mother's breast. I thought of anything simple that could capture that noise and help me avoid facing the reality that it belonged to something new.

The sound repeated, bloated and soggy, and I realised it was emanating from beneath my bed.

Gripping the rusted pole that rimmed me in for the night, I leaned over and peered into the half-foot gap of darkness. Something gleamed.

Once more I looked to the machine parts in the wall for an answer, an explanation.

The cogs turned. The pistons fired. The vents spat gas and chalky vapour.

Once more there was no answer within their workings.

With a small, shuddering breath I reached under my bed and felt something small, warm and damp. I gripped it firmly and lifted it into the diseased light that filtered in through the steel-grated ceiling above. It was one of the parts that the conveyor belt brought to me. It was all of the parts that the conveyor belt brought to me—and would bring to me forever more.

But it also wasn't.

I could feel within its bulbous red mass the difference that told me, as the etchings in the belt had told me (though in ways as yet unreachable to me), of other possibilities.

Of alternatives.

I looked up to the grated ceiling, through which I could often see the thick, buttressed legs of the supervisors as they strutted around, clipboards to their chests, but there was merely blackness up there. A blackness somehow comforting.

Protruding from the part was a tube like the ones I would place within it but with a capped ending and two tiny bars on either side. I had never seen anything like it.

Behind my eyes, for I was perhaps still partially asleep or being spoken to by the embolism, the conveyor-pattern manoeuvred. It was an infection and it was growing.

I twisted the part before me as the pattern span across my vision in a ghostly scrawl and something began to happen. A link was made that was, like everything else around me, out of my control, and in this I found some comfort for it seemed that the machines were reasserting themselves.

I crawled across the cold floor to the corner of the room where pieces of scrap metal and machine parts lay like it did throughout the factory. The machines dropped these fragments everywhere, like a mechanical shedding of skin, a rejection of diseased pieces, and they were systematically swept into corners until they were collected by workers whose tasks were not production like mine but to make possible the production when it came along. They scraped the flakes into giant bins during working time but were not due at my cell for another three shifts and so the detritus had begun to pile up.

Beyond that, however, the mess was much greater than usual.

I scrabbled around within the debris and pulled out a piece of a small cog—a semi-circle with a thick ridge of sharp teeth running the length of it. It all seemed so new all of a sudden.

Things were taking place within my mind that I knew should never be occurring and yet I was helpless to stop them. This must be the machines' wishes, I told myself for this was the only way I could comprehend the warm rush crawling up the back of my neck and around the base of my skull.

Images appeared before my eyes, the templates of which were drawn out by the conveyer-scrawl still scrolling across my vision, and my hands fast made them real, slotting metal into metal, shaft to hole, the part that had vanished from the production line the shift before and now appeared under my bed becoming lost under a mesh of wire, melted copper globules and wrinkled sheets of aluminium. In my ears there were the vague sounds of my workplace, hisses and creaks and shudders and dripping and the scream of sparks and my hands took these sounds and incorporated them into the procedure. In my mind, images of the wall before my workplace, the frailty of the steps leading away behind me, the menacing shadow of the grates that acted as a ceiling above me, the pneumatic steam firing outwards and hot red flesh emerging beneath it. And these too were taken by my hands and made metal.

My breath came hard and fast. I felt so distant, so apart from myself as the pistons fitted into my skull fired continuously in ragged bursts.

And then I was holding something new, something the size of a small human head that was covered in exposed wires, crooked bolts and broken mouldings. Blood trickled from various gashes in my hands. Sweat was gouged from my brow.

The thing was almost ball-shaped.

It almost had facial features from the way pieces stuck out variously.

It almost grinned back at me.

I turned it around and around in my hands, fascinated at this new object that wasn't anything like the parts that came to me on the production line. And yet the pipe still poked out from beneath a layer of charred gauze, it's altered ending even clearer to me now.

A capped ending and two tiny bars.

I ran one hand across the wall before me and after a yard or two felt my finger disappear into a small slot just above eye level. I drew myself closer and examined the slot. Then raised the construction to the wall and pressed it in. The pipe fitted perfectly into the jagged gap. It clicked when I twisted the construction and the two bars connected with a pair of corresponding nodes in the wall's machinery.

I let go of the construction and slid back on numbed legs.

Around it, the mechanisms continued their workings, unaffected.

The part, newly disfigured, seemed somehow happy there.

After a few moments, it began to turn, revolutions that were ragged and jerky at first but that became rapidly smoother.

It was boring itself into the wall in perfect rhythm with the rest of the machinery.

I shuddered at what was happening before me, heard the rattle of distant footsteps upon the grating above me, then hurried back across to my bed and pulled the stained and torn sheets across me. I continued to watch the mechanism integrate itself into the wall as the footsteps neared and I felt the supervisor's presence nearing.

The mechanism swung, turned, melted into the wall.

It was gone just as the shadow of the supervisor passed over my forehead.

I pressed my eyes shut and kept them that way until well after the supervisor's footsteps had faded to nothing but listened until sleep took me once more to the sound of my creation escaping into the machinery.

>in this place time is measured in shifts
>for this is how our lives revolve
>blocks of existence, arranged so the production line
>never stops

Upon my next shift, my eyes sprang open on schedule and I descended the brittle steps that took me to my workplace—and almost instantly I knew something was wrong.

The metal around me was cold and still when it should have been warming to greet me, joints groaning where the pneumatic pressure was building. The conveyor belt was moving but this never stopped, whether I was working or not because there was always someone, somewhere who was.

I stood numbly before the workplace, uncertain of what to do next.

It was then there was a great screeching noise and one of the plates of the ceiling swung down towards me. From behind it's rusted mesh a supervisor emerged, his inordinately long legs carrying him down into my zone without any need for jumping. The sockets in his hips accepted the excess thigh bone when it was no longer needed and he had reached the floor, re-routing it behind him so that two shining pistons stuck out at an angle on his lower back. His long, flowing overcoat wrapped itself around him like beetle wings, clipboard attached to one hand via a series of erratic stitches that had become infected.

His mouth parts moved as he held the contents of the clipboard up for me to see.

The document was presented in ultra-fine print too small for me to read but headed with a single word, the only word relevant to me.

REASSIGNMENT.

The supervisor reached out for me, claw fingers clinging to my uniform, and I attached myself to his wide, ridged back so that he could lift me into the above, for that was the only way out. As I was drawn through the ceiling I glimpsed another worker taking my place, his apron already full of pipes.

He looked just like me.

I was led through the crawlspace that existed between levels, in which the supervisors made their routes. I passed over worker after worker, each glimpsed through the steel mesh flooring, each devoured by the task they had been assigned to, and I began to see in their actions the continuity that been suggested by the conveyor-glyphs, to see the process that existed beyond us.

The sights and sounds were intermingling with one another, combining in ways that I knew they shouldn't. I began to lose my mind.

After three shifts in my new cell I still did not question my reassignment for it was not for me to do. However I was now experiencing a curious vacant feeling in my stomach as I stood before my new workplace. The panelling segregating me from the rest of the machine was much more efficient than that of my last workplace. It was smooth and complete, the wall before me constructed of a similar material that formed a single, uninterrupted surface. And although the sounds of mechanics-pneumatics continued behind them both the noises were soft and featureless, a drone, and for some reason this disappointed me, though I had no idea why it should. Obviously this construction was more suitable for the task I was to carry out because there could be no other reason for the difference.

Everything had to be conducive to the production.

To my left, three plastic flaps hung down over an opening in the dividing layer. They spread to make way for the part which came to me. It was larger and cleaner that the red chunks that had come to me before, with more shapes and angles but none of them ragged or malformed. I couldn't tell whether I was further along the production line, after more processes had taken place, or closer to the start, before the part had been taken apart.

There was a docile quality to the pieces that was enhanced by my task.

I was to watch the part trickle along the conveyor belt and make sure it didn't tumble onto its side.

They never did, of course, because their shape and weight meant there was only one way which they could sit and so my hands gripped the thick bar that ran lengthways before me and squeezed it rhythmically just to remain active. There was a strange itching in them to grasp, to hold, to mould and I thought at first that this was the remnants of my previous task but soon began to suspect it was something more. The desire was fading quickly, however, in my new environment and I found myself spending much time thinking about the device that had been birthed in my hands, wondering what had become of it—if it had been eaten by the greater machine and become a part of it as it had scurried around inside or if it had continued to evolve and was now its own system.

I continued to watch the scrawl on the conveyor belt as the shifts passed but this too had been cleaned and tempered into a smoother, less distinctive creature. Its expressions became softer, less angry and at times they almost became silent altogether. I began to wonder if they were choosing not to speak with me anymore, if they had been silenced or if I had imagined their previous messages and was only now seeing what was really there.

Shifts passed and I had almost forgotten about that night of creation completely when, instead of the usual controlled package of shape that I had become used to watching slide along in front of me, my device returned to

me. It was a greater being by that time, having added to itself in the form of several sprockets and a weighty, coiled
mechanism that embraced the thing, protected it, and two
masses like limbs.

My hands, having become numb to their scopophilic future, instantly seized the device from the conveyor belt before it could vanish into the other opening.

I turned the thing over and over, falling in love with its
edges, its inconsistencies, its roughness and oil-covered
severity. Tiny wheels moved within it, a hundred revolutions all taking place at once. My heart began to race and
for the first time in as long as I could remember the pistons
fitted to the side of my head fired.

The sound of the pneumatics was amazing to me in a
world that had become devoid of all noises save the constant, pressing drone of the factory.

I touched the device and with each new point of contact
another experience emerged.

> wet, cold oil kissing my fingers
> serrations too small to see, too sharp to feel their cuts
> the click of a cog tooth meeting with another
> hydraulics reacting excitedly to my touch

And suddenly the messages on the conveyor belt came
alive before me, emerging from the entrance partition with
new vigour, wildly expressive and like nothing I had wit-
nessed in them before.

One of the more complete (or incomplete) parts slid out
from under the plastic flaps and without thought I stabbed
the mechanism downwards and into its soft back. The two
connected beneath a noise disastrously near to a scream,
then a whine as I worked the disparate constructions into
some new.

The abrupt rush that had overtaken me was emptied
into my final twist as the pair locked together.

The pistons kept firing madly next to my eyes, stabbing
pain entering my chest as I struggled for air.

I was feeling something new, something amazing.

And as the mechanism was carried off by the conveyor
belt I began to see before me the wonder of all the possible
variations on what I had made. One simple connection
could be replaced by another and that piece would be

unique—unlike the one before it, in whatever minor way possible.

My hands were tingling beneath the rivulets of blood, aching for something else to be put in them so it could be raped and re-constructed.

But it was then, as the images died off, exhausted, that I became aware of the eyes above me and the moving mouth parts beside them.

I stared beyond the mesh ceiling into the darkness beyond, sweat peeling off of my forehead, my chest swelling uncontrollably, and fixed the supervisors with a questioning gaze.

Light flashed upon the metal of their clipboards and they scurried off.

I was left to the tired, but invigorated, pattern on the conveyor belt and the lonely grey silence of my workplace.

The next part arrived as it should and I watched it pass by, as was my task.

Impressions of what it could become appeared ghost-like in my head.

At the end of my shift I ascended the ramp that had replaced the steps in my old workplace and draped myself in blankets.

I dreamed of swimming in seas of mercury, of scaling barbed wire fences, of molten lead furnaces.

I had never dreamed before.   ·

Soon I stood in my workplace once more, every inch of me tingling as I awaited the first part not because of what I would do to it but of what I could do to it. Never had I sparkled and gleamed inside as I did that day.

I gripped the bar before me once more, squeezing it incessantly, my eyes wide as I gazed down at the conveyor belt.

But something was wrong.

My hold on the bar softened as I leaned forward, closer.

The glyphs continued to pass before me but I could tell they were ill.

They trickled before me awkwardly, skipping around, fading, disappearing before they were meant to.

I touched the metal with one cautious finger and felt a wave of coldness pass through me.

I looked to the plastic flaps, realising I had been standing now for almost a minute without a single part being delivered. The first was due forty-five seconds ago and they were never this late. They were never late.

Above me, the sound of something heavy pressing against the metal ceiling.

There I glimpsed more supervisors that I had ever seen before in all my shifts huddled together, their clipboards forming a pyramid at the centre of them as they watched me intently.

I had offended the machinery.

I could hear it in the way their mouth parts moved.

The sound became that of fine steel points emerging from the walls and the floor at various places, thickening as they drew outwards into great spikes three inches in diameter and of ever-increasing length. Their ends were flaking rust as they moved towards me and I realised there was nowhere to turn. I remained crouched over the conveyor belt, holding the bar as I felt the first press against me, just below my shoulder blade.

Then a whirring sound and variously-toothed spinning blades had worked their way out of the spikes, swivelling elbow-joints attaching them but giving them total freedom. One bit into my lower leg and I gritted my teeth against the pain. Another sliced at my Achilles tendon, sawing into it and spitting my blood out.

My betrayal of the machine was great and I found myself wishing for the multitude of assemblies that continued to spawn in my head would stop but it was too late, I couldn't drive them back and as I was deconstructed I watched the watchers looming over me and smiled because I was certain they didn't know where my device was or what it had become because it was mine, not theirs—it was beyond them.

I came slowly and variously apart that night, my body parts separated randomly by the blades, the spikes, the ragged edges and all the other machine pieces that had been called upon that night to perform the task of making me back into my constituent parts.

I remember what came next in blood-soaked fragments;

>being dumped piece by piece onto the conveyor belt
(who too was being punished for its betrayal)
>the plastic flaps draping me, then giving way to
>immense pipes running overhead

>a hundred workers all alike
>a place filled with tubs into which I was emptied and stirred,
>tubs which spilled themselves onto a giant metallic conveyor belt
>leaving thick blobs of organic waste which in turn were processed
>added to
>mutated
>then completed—as what they had gone in as.

For it was then that the purpose of the factory, the product which we all made and yet had no comprehension of, made itself clear to me.

We made workers to operate the factory.

As some parts of me continued to be stirred, the rest made their way along the conveyor belt where I saw my fellow workers rape me with circuit boards or weld me to hydraulics. Each one I was brought to added something new to me—polishing me, cleaning my edges, oiling my machinery—until I emerged into a huge, empty room that vanished into darkness before it ended, naked and reborn save for one vital part.

I shivered in the cold air and looked up at the same gathering of supervisors that had ordered the factory to recycle me, their buttressed lower legs entangling with one another so that they seemed to be a single, multi-headed creature.

On the concrete before me was a single, shining pipe.

The final piece of my machinery.

I lifted one arm and tucked a finger under my left breast. The skin and pectoral muscles came away easily, exposing the red, wet hole beneath in which my heart lay still. I shoved the pipe in, pressing it under the flap I could feel with the tip of my finger. An instant later, my heart began beating in perfect rhythm with the factory.

I stood and took from the supervisors the uniform that was offered to me. Over that I placed an apron whose pocket was filled with small pipes.

The gathering parted down the middle, revealing the doorway behind them which opened onto the set of frail metal steps that descended to my workplace. I heard the hiss of steam as the first part arrived and took out one of the pipes.

Without looking back I went down the steps and re-started my task, seeing now that I had been allowed the glimpses that I had of other possibilities only to show their insanity. The machine was perfect, as it always had been, the production line endless and unflawed. It built the builders, an endless stream of mass-produced gods, their own creators, their own destroyers.

There was no need for anything outside of it.

And around me, the factory hummed delicately as every inner working fitted together once more.

ignition

When she first found me my skin and clothes were sparkling from the kerosene which I had poured over myself. I held a metal pipe in one hand, ready to strike it against the concrete and spark my own ignition. The docks were almost entirely silent around us, save for the simple sounds of poisoned water lapping against the pier's steel struts and a few lone mechanisms performing their automata tasks.

She had emerged from the shadows of the huge warehouses that lay like giant bug carcasses upon the docks' concrete flooring. She was dressed in the same manner as I would come to know her for—hobnailed boots peeling at the toes to reveal their steel underskins; dark grey overalls three sizes too big for her that she wore only as far as the waist, leaving the upper half dangling like a partially-shed membrane; a dirty white tank top with a giant orange radiation sign spray-painted onto it [black bra straps fallen loose on either side]. Her oil-black hair was pinned up at the back, held in place by three thin metal spikes, loose strands curtaining her angular face. And, most importantly, she wore that softly quizzical, mildly entertained look on her face that I would come to know and hate.

She just stood there, watching, and for several minutes neither of us moved or spoke.

I felt itchy, anxious to grind the pipe against the ground but I couldn't do it with her standing there. My self-immolation was a private matter.

She made no signs that she was going to leave, however, stepping out of the shadows and into the pale light cast by the few remaining floodlights that had bulbs in them. She crossed her arms and raised an eyebrow.

"Don't mind me," she said, all honeyed-voice and liquid eyes and quiet, bubbling aggression.

I looked down at the pipe then back at her. My body was screaming for the flames that would come and possibly rescue me but my arm felt numb and useless.

Kerosene dripped from my hair and down my face, burning my skin lightly in places.

She took another step towards me.

My hand tensed around the pipe, threatening what I had gone there to do.

Her eyes narrowed as she stared intently at me. Her demeanour had already said what she then verbalised moments later.

"Do it".

The numbness that had wrapped around my arm had spread over my chest, legs and head. She was ruining *everything*. I let my eyes do my pleading for me, begging her to go.

"Do it," she repeated, grinning lightly.

I twisted the pipe against the concrete, grinding it softly.

She looked at me disdainfully. *Put some effort into it.*

Somehow it had become a challenge to see if I could go through with it. And, of course, I could. If I could handle drownings, three-hundred foot plunges, nailguns to the head and multiple wrist- and neck-slashings then I could handle immolation.

And that was exactly my problem.

My new, more annoying problem was that Shiva was watching me. The fact that someone was merely questioning my ability to go through with it was enough to make me uncertain of myself. But that's lack of self-confidence for you.

She took another step towards me, unimpressed by my efforts so far.

And, if I remember correctly, that was when she took out the lighter.

It looked to me like a welders instrument, one of those miniature soldering devices that nobody used anymore

She looked at me intently, flicking the barrel and igniting a small flame for a moment before letting it extinguish itself. Then she slid a small switch on the instrument and the flame quietly burned away without her needing to hold it down.

I hesitated, then twisted the pipe a little harder. It sparked but didn't catch.

I momentarily wondered if the kerosene had soaked in too deep or dried off and that there wouldn't be enough left to carry out the task. How embarrassing.

The flame coming from her lighter glowed blue-bright in the night air, threatening.

She took another step towards me.

Strange that I should feel fear. What she was threatening was exactly what I had come here to do—why should I be scared of her or what she would do?

Maybe it wasn't fear but territorialism. This was my body and if it was going to be destroyed then it should be me who did it.

At the time, I hadn't even considered why she would *want* to do this to me, to assist in the conflagration of a total stranger.

Another step and she was mere feet away from me - *inches* from the puddle of kerosene that surrounded me. And still with that lighter burning away.

A smile crept across her face as my hand began to loosen involuntarily on the pipe. What was she *doing* to me?

The thought was just finishing when she threw the lighter at my feet and the fuel I had draped myself in burst into flames, taking me with it.

I remember seeing her eyes wide with pleasure as I glimpsed her, through the watery air that spread around the inferno I had become.

Some time later we sat crouched on the low roof of a storage building in the heart of the collection of poison-manufacturing plants that had become known as Plague Central. Insane structures rose all around us in pitch-black night, architecturally bizarre constructs that were built specifically to funnel toxic fumes and chemicals from one plant to the next like giant concrete junkies sharing the contents of their needles. There were rusted warning signs everywhere, posted on walls and doors, poles and windows.

Danger—Noxious chemicals. Oxygen masks must be worn at all times.

No admittance during daylight hours.

Authorised personnel only.

Most were cracked and faded, almost unreadable. Some had come loose from their fixings and swung from the final remaining bolt. Others had been sprayed with graffiti.

Shiva took off her backpack and opened it. There was a tangible charge of anticipation surrounding the two of us as she removed the three devices she has spent the past few days constructing.

I glanced cautiously over the low wall that encircled the roof top, watched two workers dressed in full chemical suits, complete with double-filtered gas masks, as they passed below us. They carried between them a pneumatic trolley loaded with a low, wide drum with a radiation sign stamped on it.

My stomach had begun acting up again the day before and it now felt like I had swallowed a puffer fish that was slowly expanding itself into a football-sized lump of spikes deep inside me. I longed to curl up into myself and scream away the pain. I wondered if perhaps what Shiva and I had been doing the past month or so didn't really ease the pain any after all—that I was just distracted from it.

"Here, put this on," she instructed, handing me the harness she had made earlier in the week. It consisted of several combat belts welded together at their buckles so that it embraced me around the chest, waist and neck. There were three slots, two small iron chambers the size of a pint bottle on either of my hips and one larger one on the back [the latter being a modified oxygen tank rack]. Once I had gotten the thing on she clipped the devices she had removed from her backpack into the slots, twisting them so that they clicked and locked in place.

I'm pretty sure she considered her bomb-making an art form. She spent hours sketching designs and circuitry diagrams for them in her workshop while I attempted to ease my stomach pains by consuming whatever drugs she had found for me. While I spat blood into the cracked bowl of her bathroom sink I listened to the sound of her working; the drills, the hiss of solder, the screech of metal being beaten into shape. She spent as much time on the aesthetics of the devices as the inner workings, sculpting smooth, rounded casings out of polymers she softened with heat. And as I came to understand her a little more I saw that she enjoyed endlessly perfecting these mechanisms not *in spite* of the fact that she knew they were going to be destroyed but *because* of it.

She turned me around to double-check the largest bomb was securely strapped into place in the oxygen tank rack, then back again so that I faced her. Her eyes were wide and gleeful, shining. From her backpack she took a small handful of grenades and clipped them to the strap that ran across my chest then leaned back to admire her work.

"Beautiful," she said. "Are you ready?"

I nodded, then winced as a bolt of pain lanced through my stomach.

"Is it getting worse?" she asked. I assumed the concern in her voice was that we might not successfully complete the mission—not for any suffering I might be going through.

"Bearable," I told her.

"Good." She touched a button on each of the devices, initiating their timers. She zipped up her backpack again and slipped it over her shoulders. "Give me a couple of minutes to get clear."

She smiled at me somewhere between a fat carnivore looking at a freshly-boiled hog and an art-lover looking at an original Monet. I don't know which made me feel more degraded.

Then she had turned and was sprinting across the rooftops. She leapt with the same feline quality that described her every physical feature, dropping effortlessly on the other side of eight-foot gaps. I watched her until she reached the very edge of the compound, until she leapt onto the razor-wire fencing, the heavy welding gloves she wore protecting her precious hands.

When she was gone, everything seemed as still and quiet as it always did, perhaps because I was already thinking about the cacophony that would soon follow. I looked down at one of the bombs locked onto my hip, at the red LCD display rapidly sliding towards zero.

2:06

She always started the timers, never me. I had learned long before I met her that, for whatever reason, I was no longer able to control my own life or death—so perhaps I wanted to see if someone else could.

I enjoy this time before the destruction begins, when things are peaceful and my stomach pains fade with all sounds. But it's always over so quickly.

I checked the timers then got to my feet. I crouched over the roof's low wall and saw a number of suited workers attending to their tasks. I took one of the grenades from my chest strap and removed the pin with a flick of my thumb. A second after one of the workers heard the pin clatter against the ground I threw the grenade down and jumped after it.

It hit the wall of the building opposite and in a split second the palm-sized lump of metal and chemicals became a billowing cloud of fire and smoke and flaming particles. The explosion caught me full-on and threw me back towards the rooftop I came from, slamming me into the wall just short of the roof. I crumpled to the ground and it was then I heard the screaming begin.

Through a wall of flames I glimpsed frenzied movements, limps bodies. I got to my feet a little unsteadily and ran at the fire, ran through it. One of the workers was on fire so I threw another grenade at his feet to put him out of his misery. I leapt to one side to avoid the main thrust of the blast, which demolished almost half of the wall of the building he stood next to. I saw him thrown backwards into the collapsing concrete, instantly buried under a fragment that disintegrated his face, his chest, his lower legs.

I hurried over a pair of bodies slumped against each other and ran towards a dome-like construction some way ahead. I retrieved another grenade from my harness and flipped the pin. There was an immense crash as the building behind me gave way, taking with it the transmission tower which had once been atop it. A siren suddenly sounded as blue lights began flashing all around me.

1:30

More workers were spilling out of labs and research dens, most suited but the rest merely dressed in white smocks or lab coats. Some saw me, this mad bomber loaded with explosives. Others only saw the rapid chain of explosions that were triggering each other off.

The air was quickly filling with poisonous fumes and purple-black smoke.

I jumped at the dome and scurried up it's slanted side, removed one of the bombs from my hip and dropped it into a vent in the roof. There was a sudden roar of flame from beside me as a chemical tank exploded; boiling hot gases threw me from the dome and I slammed into the concrete, feeling my shoulder pop put of place. I gritted my teeth and got up once more, threw another grenade into the near distance and then ducked as it went off, sending scientist-bodies through the air like pure white cherry blossoms.

The sirens went silent, the generator that powered them having been crushed under the weight of a satellite dish from the neighbouring blockade falling onto it, leaving only the blue warning lights flickering over the destruction, strobing it so that it seemed to occur in slow motion.

I imagined myself to look almost ghostlike as I raced through the compound within that stuttering blue illumination, my movement only partially described by it. Another two grenades thrown either side of me and I jumped just in time to allow myself to be carried forward by the blast a hundred times faster than I could have managed unassisted. This was what I had learned in my time with Shiva and her bombs—not to fear the destruction but to live inside it, to become a part of it. She said that we too were an explosion ripping through mortar and steel and glass; we were human bombs igniting everything around us.

I scurried up a fallen communications tower, using it like a ladder to get onto the roof of a higher building, one whose roof was a pool of flames. I ran to the catwalk that extended out across it and over a courtyard filled with drums of all shape and sizes, dropped my other hip bomb as I went.

0:40

Then leapt at the lab on the other side as the catwalk's metal frame fell away from under me, sheared in half by a chunk of concrete ejected from the midst of a smaller explosion somewhere to my left.

In this world of the explosive, I hear screams and the shattering of glass. The boom of giant structures slamming into the ground and the screeching of metal being torn apart. I smell petroleum and noxious chemicals but within it is always something sweet which I think may be burning flesh and I think may be my own. I feel the intangible ripples that crease the air like the aftershocks of an earthquake and the acidic bite of the flames.

0:15 and I had reached the back of the compound. The chaos Shiva and I had created was complete. The world was collapsing into a fireball around me, dust clouds and shattered concrete pillars and there, in between two corrugated iron shacks housing bottle after bottle of all manner of poisons, I knelt down. I had outrun the destruction and was left to a gentle peace, the air around me warmed by the fires now burning furiously in the near distance.

0:08

I felt the remaining few seconds dribbling out of the LCD display on the final device as if they were the liquid crystal itself. The other two I had planted were set to go off simultaneously, a triangular assault set to reduce the whole compound to ashes and jagged rubble. I curled into a ball, breathed once, ready for the ignition of the forty-three pounds of explosives and flammable potions strapped to my scarred back and hoped that perhaps this time it would take me into the pyroligneous aftermath along with everything else.

0:00

We are both in her workshop, her home. It is a large, mostly empty open-plan room in the only remaining stable floor of abandoned warehouse near the docks I had one day not long ago been standing in, doused in kerosene and self-hatred. (Not, not self-hatred. I never hated myself. I just didn't care either way. Self-apathy?) We lie on the dirty mattress she uses as a bed in a corner of the floor, a bedroom described only by the wire mesh screen she has constructed to cordon it off. A kerosene lamp burns by our feet.

Shiva sits on the edge of the mattress as I lie foetally curled beside her, doubled up in pain from stomach cramps that feel as if my gut has been filled with broken glass and nails. She has removed the pins from her hair so that it is rolled out down her back, almost to her waist and vaguely oriental in quality. She is smeared in engine oil and grease from her work that night.

She doesn't touch me—we never touch– but her closeness is an attempt to soothe me. I think that only now is she finally beginning to understand how debilitating these agonies are for me, months after I had revealed to her that they were the very reason I had been about to set fire to myself when she had found me [and the reason behind all the previous attempts at my own destruction].

She hands me a piece of sheet glass on which is a line of lumpy-grey powder, a concoction of analgesics she has stolen or found that she has ground up for me. Next to the line is a thin metal pipe no larger than 1 centimetre in diameter which I use as a straw to inhale the medicine, needing two attempts since I can't move off of my side.

My wounds are healing as quickly as ever, any pain they might be subjecting me to lost in the miasma of hot stabs and burning sensations coming from my stomach as if the organ itself were melting within me. At first the remedies she fed me helped almost as much as the cleansing fires but now they seemed to barely touch the pain. In fact it is worse than it ever has been before.

I snort every last molecule of the stuff up in vain hope.

And I think, as I lie there, of that place I know so well now, that world of flames. I think of the voices I often heard in there and then of Shiva emerging from the smoke and aftermath to collect me and load me into her pick-up truck—and always with that tone to her actions that was half exhilaration and half disappointment that I had made it out again.

I don't think she *wanted* me to die. She just didn't care if I did.

So that made two of us—which was fine by me.

[an aside: In the flames, in the fire, in the heat, nothing is real, everything is described by arcs of brilliant God-like light that buries itself deep within you, illuminates all the cancers, the bad cells, the poisons, the degradations. My bodily systems are charged, frenetic, the explosions rippling around me twisting me, turning me, flipping me over and I am completely in their control, there is nothing left for me in this place of fire as I am carried forth on billowing clouds of weapons-grade napalm smoke, I am wafer-thin, like a slice of pure silicon ready to be stamped with circuitry. I am a great wet bird and this is a flammable Heaven, I am a fallen angel, my pain is no longer an option here as I fly, fly, and burn, burn, burn, I have never felt so dead and so pure and so ugly and so wonderful FUUUUCCCKKK!!!!!!! end]

On the first mission she had wrapped a thirteen-foot length of durable steel wire around my entire body. Attached to the wire in five-or-six centimetre spacings were small lumps of Semtex and some other explosive gum that was vaguely purple in colouring. Bolted to a light aluminium plate that hung from a collar around my neck like a tight-fitting bib was the trigger mechanism that would ignite me. It consisted of a small see-through tube filled with kerosene with an iron rod dipping into it and several electrical wires wrapped around it, connected to the circuit points against which the steel wire had been soldered.

So on that first night I had found myself walking into the decaying headquarters of some aged corporation that had once spread its electronic limbs from coast to coast but now lay curled up in a brittle ball like a dying spider. I wore a long coat and, in the tradition of all good suicide bombers, removed it upon entering the lobby to clearly display my weaponry.

Then all I had to do was walk from one end of the building to the other, past derelict offices and the odd employee as small explosions were triggered off on me, getting up whenever I was knocked down by their force or stray pieces of masonry. (I was more resistant to pain and injury than any properly functioning individual but was still subject to the laws of gravity). I began to run towards the end of the building as the fires that raged around me closed in, squeezing me along that last corridor and I felt, for the first time in as long as I could remember, *exhilaration*. I leapt out of the window Shiva had instructed me to just as its frame and surrounding wall blew out.

Any agreement we had made to work together like this was purely tacit.

I think it consisted of her view that she had saved my life and I was therefore owe her [she didn't fully understand my condition at this time though she must have realised that saving the life of a suicidal didn't really count at all]; it consisted of my own curiosity to see that if I was unable to kill myself then perhaps she *would* be, since she was putting much more effort into it than I ever had; and it consisted of the fact that she provided me with relief from my stomach pains from the pills she scavenged from god-knows-where.

At first I had not questioned Shiva's intentions—why she wanted to destroy what she did.

She was an anarchist, after all, so for a time I had merely assumed she was destroying for the sake of it. She seemed to have a penchant for institutions and always chose places, not people, for our missions but beyond that I didn't attempt to uncover *why* she wanted them annihilated. I began to wonder if it was my *own* destruction that she sought and that the places she sent me to were therefore inconsequential. When I saw a pattern in the attacks—that each one got subsequently more dangerous, from three-hundred foot high electricity pylons to chemical labs to toxic waste plants—it was a pattern which pointed to an effort on her part to see how far my indestructibility went.

It would have been simpler for her just to ask me.

It was some months down the line, as we sat in her workshop, before I flat out asked her.

"Why do you do it?"

She didn't look up from her work at first. She was crouched over a fish tank full of chemicals as clear as mountain water, the kind you fantasise about pouring down your throat when you are dying of thirst. She had been taking more of an interest in liquid explosives the previous weeks and had been trying out differing concoctions with a view to fitting me out with translucent polymer veins full of them so that we could more adequately control the destruction.

[an aside :She often walked a fine line between control and chaos, one which I believe she was well aware of. She would spend weeks perfecting a device then at the last minute add in some random element with no idea as to how it would affect the overall outcome. Several times I found myself standing impotently in the middle of a building or factory, the explosives having failed—and several times I found myself being launched hundreds of feet into the air by a blast that went far beyond anything either us had imagined. end]

She put down the industrial-sized pipette she held, pulled her safety goggles down off her face so that they hung around her neck. Her skin was as white as a streak of hot lightning and seemed to shine in the reflective glow of what lay in the tank. She wore a different top than usual, this one light grey with a skull-and-crossbones motif sprayed onto it. The skull had X's for eyes as if it were stoned.

"I don't know—why do *you* do it?"

She put her goggles back on and went back to work, turning on the old lumpy radio she had on her workbench beside her and filling the air with useless static. I took the hint and left it there.

I waited until we had just finished a mission a few weeks later to try the question again as she was always in a better mood then. I lay in the back of her flatbed next to rusted motor engines that she had torn out of abandoned vehicles and plastic sacks full of miscellaneous circuitry. I was smoking slightly and more than a little singed. I'd also fractured four bones in my left hand.

She dabbed me with a cloth soaked in chemically-enhanced H_2O.

We were both still breathing laboriously from the buzz of the mission.

"There's no fun in destroying what you hate," she told me when I'd posed the question again. She removed a piece of circuit board from her pocket and placed my damaged hand upon it, using it as a splint which she tied into place with plastic thread. "Destroy what you love."

Then she ranted for a few minutes in her usual manner, about bureaucracy and chaos and apathy, stuff I had heard time and time again from her in smaller splinters. But that first statement stuck with me, more lucid than perhaps anything she had ever said to me before.

It was, of course, the only theme in our deviant relationship—the destruction of things.

Of things around us. Of things inside us. Of each other.

It didn't matter.

Destruction was the single most powerful force in the universe, she said. It was the natural force, the one which the cosmos itself followed for, eventually, it crushed whatever it created. It was only human beings who sought to contradict this natural law in trying to preserve things and she wanted to teach me to move beyond that.

That chemical plant we bombed the other month, where I almost broke my back when that catwalk collapsed under me—that was where she used to work as a senior technician. The job had been arranged for her after she'd been released from the asylum she'd spent some time in. They'd given her purpose, money, the freedom to express her mechanical creativity—taken the razor from her wrists in more than one sense.

I think destroying those who had helped her was the only way she was able to express her gratitude.

The first mission, I later found out, had been to the decrepit corporate headquarters of Robert Rabinowitz, the benefactor who had sponsored her life outside the asylum. He'd become like a father to her though they only ever spoke on the phone. Unlike other benefactors, he was happy to remain in the background and let her get on with her new life.

The rest had been carers, psychiatrists, fellow technicians that had moved on to better things—the places they worked for, the places they lived.

Her list went on and I followed it completely.

A method of mayhem.

Except that any method, by definition, could not be *true* mayhem, *true* chaos. That was where the x-factor came into play. That was why she had been adding poison to my stomach mixture almost since she had begun giving it to me.

The x-factor was also why I had continued to take the stuff even after I saw her secretly adding the venom through hands clenched over my face in pain. It was why I let her destroy my fragile stomach even though the pain was becoming unbearable.

Or maybe *because* the pain was becoming unbearable.

It was a further little experiment upon my life.

Then I decided to try a little experiment myself.

I smiled as I watched her shivering beside me. There was a light rain smothering the sky tonight, each drop with that faint yellow tinge and warm kiss that signalled vague acidic content.

"Are you sure you still want to go ahead with this?" I challenged gently.

"Of course," she said and gave me one of those looks of hers like she was some sort of childish demon. Her hair lay in scrappy tufts around her face now and had uneven streaks of luminous colour washed through it. She'd made the change after I had told her that I liked how straight and death-black it was.

I'd helped her do it.

We both clung to the steel shafts and criss-crossing girders of the tower we were climbing as the rain grew heavier.

It was a relay station for the emergency signals the asylum she had been in used when patients' lives were in danger, the only link to specialist medical teams that she had more than once had working on her (after she had worked on herself).

The bombs we carried rattled against the metal and against each other. They were little more than simple grenades this time, though filled with corrosive acids. I think she had been too preoccupied with the challenge I had presented to her to come up with anything more creative.

I had pointed out to her, one night the previous week, that she could not know chaos until she had lived within it. Creating it by proxy, through the protective shield of another being, and then watching what followed safely from a distance—that wasn't anarchy.

We had both been drunk at the time and high on toxins but I was lucid enough to see the opportunity to start my experiment and she was wasted enough to fall into it (though I suspect her response would have been the same had she been stone-cold sober). There was only one possible response for her if I challenged her dedication to destruction.

So she remained beside me as I climbed and I could see the glimmer in her eye, the fear slipping away as she got closer to her own death. It was an utterly liberating experience, to know that you could die at any moment and not give a shit.

Two hundred and fifty feet into the swirling air in the dead of night with someone who might just give you the shove into the spiralling ground-mass you know you are just one step away from—now *that's* living.

"We can do it from here," she said when we were about three quarters of the way up.

I stared right back at her. The question of what would happen when the first explosive was set off and the tower began to collapse beneath us had been left untouched by both of us.

I kept climbing and after a slight pause she chased me up, overtaking me on the other side as the struts came together. A warped and defective satellite dish was perched on the apex, lolling uselessly in the strong winds.

So there we were, atop a three hundred foot tower which, in turn, was atop a sixty-foot high bunker surrounded by loose razorwire, about to blow it all away from under us. I leaned across and hit the trigger switch on her chest which was fused to all the bombs and started her countdown. She did the same for me.

0:10

And we stared silently at each other.

Shared death, or the impedance thereof, offers a bond which cannot be found anywhere else. There can be only one who looks into your eyes in your final moment as you look back.

0:07

Fuck you I mouthed.

0:04

Fuck you back she mouthed in return, then grinned and screamed at the air with a mutant breed of joy.

0:01

And then the explosions began and the tower was wrenched apart, taking us with it and we fell, we fell together, thrown like pieces of stray garbage as metal seared past us and slammed into us and then, through flames and shattered steel and chemical air, we hit the ground.

She had almost died that night, having impaled herself on a fractured rod of iron just to the left of her kidney.

I never went on a mission alone again.

[an aside: In truth, chaos is a blend of multiple orders all mixed and intertwined with each other. Order can only exist on the smallest, most superficial of scales—anything beyond that and you can see the cracks, the fault lines, the irrationalities. Chaos *consumes* order without annihilating it. It allows it to continue but works its spidery fingers so that each order is wrapped around another conflicting one, the other's mere presence enough to contradict the perfection of the first.

Iodine crystals, ammonium hydroxide, potassium iodide, sodium thiosulfate (aka photographic hypo), granular explosives, ammonia, kerosene, rubbing alcohol, salt, sugar, petroleum, fixing agents, binding agents, semtex, rubber putty, moulding wires, electrical tape, 90cc, 120cc, 4.3 grams mixed with 0.8 grams, liquid solutions, ammonium nitrogen tri-iodide, gelatine capsules, touch paper, sodium azide, lead nitrate, potassium chlorate, aluminium dust, lampblack, glycerine, sodium peroxide, gum arabic, me, Shiva.

All bound together under chaos. end]

Running alongside her like that added something new
to it all.

It was part company, part invasion of my own privacy,
her being there.

It was lonely amongst the explosions but then loneliness never really bothered me. When I put a gun to my
head and pulled the trigger two years ago it wasn't out of
loneliness that I did so.

I found myself igniting the strips of razor-thin alco-
hol-soaked plastic she attached to us only when she was
near. I found myself arcing grenades close enough to risk
catching her in the blast. I found myself switching the
timer mechanisms on before we had planned to, forcing
her to sprint ahead of me to get out of range before they
went off.

I enjoyed knowing how much more vulnerable than me
she was to it all.

Our time together felt more exhilarating than it ever had
before.

Soon, and probably in response to my own increasing
disregard for her life, Shiva began testing my impervious-
ness to the limits, adding more explosives, more corro-
sives, more concentrated trigger liquids to the mechanisms I carried. (For although she came with me it was still
I who was burdened with the fearsome machinery she
built). And by then it was no longer about the buildings
and structures that we were destroying; as I had been previously suspicious of, by then she was selecting targets at a
whim merely so that we could prolong this experiment
with our own mortality. She ceased telling me why we
were attacking the places that we went to and I ceased ask-
ing.

She also upped the levels of the poisons she added to
the mixtures she fed me to heal a stomach now so badly
torn and disintegrated that it barely existed at all. I could-
n't eat or drink anything or even smell food; it was painful
to breathe.

One night I challenged her further. She had snapped a
tendon in the back of her knee after a girder had fallen
across her and as she wrapped it in a splint I offered her
some of the grey-green powder she had left out for me. We
looked at each other and I could see in her eyes that she

knew I was aware of what she had been doing. I placed my straw onto the glass and snorted and seconds later felt as if I had just inhaled hot, wet tarmac. Then I offered the straw to her.

Her face, previously creased with pain, softened.

She knew. I knew. We both knew.

She snorted up every last speck and didn't flinch.

And so we both ran, headlong, into nihilism and oblivion as our experimentation with each other continued. Hatred for hatred, tick-tock timers, the liquid fire of ignition, the snap of the mechanisms firing, her fury, my fury and steel-and-glass temples razed to the ground.

We had become like DNA strands coiled around each other.

We were loaded with ammunition and we destroyed everything in sight except the one thing that we wanted to.

Sometimes I watched her while she slept.

Her hair was back to around shoulder-length but still scrappy and lined with streaks of red and blue and white and it hung to one side of her face. The curve of her back was a perfect arc like the line my grenades would fall through. If I were to taste it, her skin it would remind me of mallow. The scars that littered her body made her look, in the glow of the phosphor mixture she left to burn now that we had run out of decent fuel, like an Egyptian parchment with some deviant message etched upon it. Something to do with gods and stars and cool blue oceans.

I wondered what I would do without her.

I had learned enough in our time together to create rudimentary bombs—nothing like she could make but probably satisfactory. And there was always a reason to destroy some new target.

So I didn't need her for her expertise or her grand plan. I didn't really need her at all anymore. She'd served her purpose. I could slash her throat while she slept or, to be poetic, douse her in kerosene and set her alight. I could throw one of the bombs she gave me right at her instead of to one side as we ran, ran, ran. Or while the timer on a device dropped to 5 seconds I could blow her legs away from under her so that she lay beside me as I went off.

But instead I watched her as she slept.

One night she opened her eyes suddenly and caught me.

I'd become complacent in my voyeurism, used to the deep, heavy sleep that she fell into each night. There was nothing else for me to do but to keep looking at her.

She stared back and probably saw it in my eyes.

And we both knew the experiment was over.

Soon after, Shiva began collecting as much of the raw materials she used as she could.

Much was scavenged from the warehouses around us but most was stolen from factories and workshops further into the city. I went with her in these mini-missions, plugging explosive putty laced with ammonium nitrate into cracks in walls then clicking a hand-trigger to tear the concrete apart, then waiting as she strolled in, grabbed what we needed and loaded it into the pickup.

We rarely spoke the whole time.

She came back one night with the biggest plastic sack of iodine crystals I had ever seen. It took us an hour to wipe her skin with sodium thiosulfate to get the stains off.

The sack was followed with dynamite sticks, car batteries, gallon tanks of lab-strength ammonium sulphate and peroxide, bags of dry putty mixture, bars of solid lead and iron to be melted down and clear glass bottles containing acids I couldn't recognise. She worked constantly and with an aggression to her movements that unnerved me slightly as she grazed vats of pre-mixed chemicals with trigger threads which she was carrying or lit flames mere feet from small piles of magnesium compounds (which only made things more interesting).

Throughout that time, the longest period in which we had not been out since we had come together save for the mini-missions for the ingredients, I sat on the mattress with the screen pulled aside and watched her. I had difficulty sitting upright by this point, my stomach screaming hot fire whenever it was stretched slightly and I felt as if it might well split in two if I moved suddenly, so I lay on one side, my hand beneath my face. I often passed out to the sound of her steel toecaps ringing off of the floor or to the hiss of her blowtorch.

The framework to her latest mechanism began to become noticeable by the third week and it was huge. The skeleton was formed by interlocking bars of thick, scarred steel that began in the far corner of the room, near the grimy windows that looked out onto the docks, and mutated in shape back and forth until it almost reached the mattress where I lay. The spinal column was a series of conical tanks welded together, stacked atop one another and each containing variously coloured liquid that was stirred continuously by black rods.

It began to hum and tick a few days later—it was both clockwork and electrical.

A dark energy surrounded the two of us, crackling and ugly like stale light bulbs.

And while she worked I felt as if I might finally be dying. I had become skeletal, having not eaten for over a month, but more importantly having not been within the world of flames and ignition for three weeks. My stomach pains clouded my perceptions of the device which was growing around me so that I occasionally believed it to be a giant arachnid leering over me.

She sat next to me one evening and assembled around twenty palm-sized mines that looked like the black teardrops of a humpback whale. She looked at me occasionally but didn't say a word. There was excitement in her eyes; and hurt and anger.

Every eighteen hours or so she poured a liquid version of her poisoned medicine down my throat because I didn't have the strength to sniff it up anymore then drank some herself. I wondered if she even bothered putting anything else other than the toxins into it any more (the blood she vomited regularly and the skull-like appearance her face had assumed attested to this).

Industrial-sized cans of chemicals circled the room, inch-thick electrical cord dipping into them and then out again. The whole room stank of chlorine. I have a memory of hearing Shiva crying, but only for a moment. There were hisses—sharp and fast from the pneumatics she had fitted onto the mechanism, long and soft from the vents in the top of bubbling vats.

Then, finally, she sat next to me on the mattress.

Strapped to her back was a device that looked somewhat like a one-armed bandit that had been dumped and left to rust. Out of either side emerged two large rubber coils that were attached to sockets in the bomb she had built around us.

She pulled my limp body into her lap and that was the first and last time she would ever touch me.

Then she unclipped two triggers from the her pack. They looked like fat lighters with a simple on/off switch on one end and a wire extending from the other around her back, presumably into the device there. She placed one in the palm of my hand and held the other in her own.

This is what you've done to us her eyes said. And then (maybe); *thank you.*

The whole room hummed with the energy of the bomb-construct. My throat was clogged with bloody phlegm that I couldn't spit out. I noticed she'd died her hair pitch black again and left it to grow out.

"Together," she said softly and placed her thumb on the switch.

I parroted the gesture and there were several moments of a strange, alien silence between us before we flicked the switches in unison.

Just inside my line of sight a one-by-four foot LCD display mounted onto the wall lit up in bright green lettering.

0:60

0:59

0:58

0:57

I looked into her eyes - Shiva, the Destroyer Of All, the final being in the Hindu Trimurti—and there was too much going on in them to decipher what she was feeling or thinking.

Had we come this far? Had we come to this moment, here, now?

We were in a building filled with enough explosives to take out the entire warehouse district with us, enough to bring a thousand dead fish to the surface if there had actually been any left alive. We had come together; we had fallen apart; we had come together.

I just wanted to know what she was feeling, if she was angry or hurt or ecstatic. I wanted to know that I mattered enough to her that she would kill us for it or that I mattered so *little* that she would kill us for it.

But, of course, she wasn't killing *us*.

0:43

0:42

0:41

I would awaken, in the rubble, in the flames—and she wouldn't be there to load me into her truck. I would be free of her again. She had failed me, failed herself in her attempts to murder me. Or I had failed me, us. This was the agony of when I was twelve and I swallowed the vial of battery acid I had extracted from my father's car that began the disintegration of my stomach because I didn't care if I fizzled away there and then (or twelve years later).

0:32

Do you want to live? I wanted to ask her. *Is that why you're doing this? Because you don't want it? Because I don't want it?*

0:22

Of course it was—there was no other reason for us.

0:13

And then I saw, in her eyes what she really felt. I began to ache more than I ever had during my miserable life.

0:07

I saw apathy.

0:04

She didn't give a shit either way if we lived or died.

0:01

And that was the most terrible thing I could imagine.

0:00

Ignition.

foetal chambers

They are held in one of a series of tanks that measures 16ft by 14ft, a near-square, in an underground chamber that is mostly concrete pillars. Black netting hangs from the tops of the pillars to disguise the abnormally high ceiling and catch the pigeon shit that drops from the rafters high above. In most places, the netting bulges with the weight of what appears to be single, solid globules of flecked white faeces.

The tanks consist of several panels of glass held together by shining steel braces so that you can look in should you wish. They are arranged in neat rows and each are, effectively, their own biosphere.

Inside them a solution of three-dozen chemicals severs the genetic ties of whatever is put in there and gives the DNA free reign. 50,000 volt electric pulses are administered every four hours to encourage the base matter's re-assembly, predictably into something new and usually awful.

Some of the creatures that float in the tanks resemble small dogs that have melted under the sun, the flaps of their skin drooping into irregular, flaccid wings. Others are as perfectly shaped as bottle-nosed dolphins, only half the size.

Lids of criss-crossing rods of metal are clamped to the top of each tank to stop its inhabitants from climbing out. These lids, and the steel braces, act as a complete circuit to hem the genetic babies in and encourage the 50,000 volts to be evenly spread when I bring down the mighty lever that controls the charges.

They would never have let me near the lever a few months ago, not before I became an Assistant Project

Leader. It's not as important as it sounds—there are twelve APL's in a department that has only twenty-five staff total—but it's important enough for me to leave behind my old duties of mopping up the spillages and wiping down the glass. Now I pull the lever that encourages new forms of life.

The other APL's gather in the recuperation room between shifts, huddling together like street vagrants trying to warm each other. I usually stand in the opposite corner with a mug of hot vitamins, staring at my feet. I don't expect them to be accepting of me considering the way I got the job.

Occasionally, the Project Leader will visit us. She is currently overseeing about a dozen separate experiments which are part of her master thesis, of which our department is a mere limb. She speaks to the others first, going over the results they have been scribbling down on their clipboards, bowing repeatedly to each other in a traditional Japanese manner.

Then she comes to me and I can feel the rest of them watching us. She does not speak to me but often touches me softly and scribbles something down on the miniature notepad strapped to her wrist. Geniuses such as the Project Leader are in a state of constant inspiration and resolution and she never seems to go more than a few minutes without jotting some equation or lateral statement on her notepad or whatever surface is available.

Our research centre is littered with this graffiti. In chalk, in marker pen, in ballpoint, in squeezed lines of condiment; mathematical puzzles and solutions, philosophical statements, stray words from two dozen different languages, diagrams, designs, endless, endless.

I often see the others peering at these markings in an attempt to decipher them. I think they would uproot the Project Leader if they could, dethrone her and leave her in the gutter as they stepped up onto her pedestal—as I once tried.

They do not know how intelligent the Project Leader is.

She visits my cell on occasion, once the strip lighting has faded for the night, its constant and erratic buzz like a malfunctioning pacemaker silenced. She must be very quiet so that the others do not hear her, though there is surely nothing they could, or would dare, do if they caught her.

She sits on the edge of my mattress and removes her clothes, then removes mine. She pulls the sheets over us and together our deformities join like pieces of an interlocking puzzle. Our skins warm each other as we lie, in peace, in silence.

They say the Project Leader has fully enabled her own alienation and can survive without the closeness of another. I know this to be true, but also know that you can never separate from the pieces of yourself that you hate.

You cannot become alien to yourself.

Of course they all know I am different, that is plain for all to see. Their animosity is directed as equally to my more obvious divergences (my misshapen head, my pitch black eyes, my awkward posture, my cracked skin) than my lesser ones (my long, dark hair, my breasts).

But only one of them looks at me deeply enough to go beyond these superficialities. Whilst the others rub their shaven heads and make ticks and crosses on their clipboards, he eyes me strategically. He wears heavy plastic-rubber gloves to protect himself when he stirs chemicals into the foetal chambers and always rolls a test tube around in one hand with latent agility, from finger to finger to finger, as he studies me.

I turn to the equipment-loaded wall on which the lever is mounted and bring the mighty pole down. The room turns purple-blue and great clouds of steam suddenly arise from the tanks for a pre-set period as the charge courses through them and the birds beyond the netting go wild. And still I feel his eyes upon me.

It has been almost three months since I was appointed to the project team in which time he has said nothing to any of the others, nor to the Project Leader. And yet I remain fearful that he will tell someone about that night he watched me emerge from one of the foetal chambers, dripping the fluids he himself had been adding to the tanks ever since the research began.

The lever ascends by nature of a clockwork mechanism, returning to its original upright position at exactly the time it is meant to. It clicks into place and in one sudden moment the light fades and the sounds of boiling water cease. There is only a gentle hiss as the last wisps of steam rising from the tanks and then the clamour of footsteps as the Primary Researchers move towards the foetal chambers to record the results.

And as I turn, my task finished until the next charge is needed, I see that he is still watching me, perched atop a drum of chemical waste like some kind of mechanical gargoyle.

As I lie beneath the Project Leader, a cancer that she has expelled from herself only to find that she cannot live without, our breathing perfectly matched, she lifts slightly from me. She sweeps her hair to one side so that it hangs down her neck and tickles my breasts. She strokes my stomach maternally and a touch of pleasure runs through me as our hips meet.

She sees the concern in my eyes, the fear that the project that birthed me is at risk and, in turn, my own existence. The Project Leader removes a stick of charcoal from her wrist pad and begins to scribble on the wall next to us. The equation is partly Ancient Greek mathematical symbols, partly binary code.

She works for a little over a minute then stops suddenly. She copies the final solution down onto her wrist pad then lowers herself onto me again.

The next day, in the recuperation room, our project team is about to commence another shift. I sit on the edge of a plastic-moulded chair, warming myself with a mug of vitamin solution that I have not taken a single sip from. My stomach feels ugly and sore, unwilling to digest even the simplest of foodstuffs.

I feel more separate than ever from the rest of them for there is a new team member—a replacement Fluid Supervisor—and he converses easily with the others even though he only arrived that morning.

We quickly return to work and I stand by the power lever as I listen to the birds flapping around above us. It seems that yesterday's charge produced a vaster acceleration in the evolution of our hybrid species than had been expected so I wait patiently as the results are recorded. The project team's excitement makes me feel more at ease as the slightly deviant physical and psychological nature of the new Fluid Supervisor goes unnoticed.

I stare confidently back as he sits perched on the chemical drum and watches me. There is a blankness in his eyes now, unlike his predecessor, the accusations and threats gone. Those things, they are now little black fish floating in the foetal chambers, a brand new life form whose base matter was knowledge that should never have been.

At one point during the work the Project Leader enters to survey this latest success. The black fish are pointed out to her and the significance of the fact that they have spontaneously appeared in each separate tank is repeatedly pointed out to her. She nods and scribbles notes on the chamber glass, on her wrist pad.

She affords me only one simple glance during the entire ten-minute visit.

The others soon leave her to examine the species by herself, returning to the workstations scattered around the room.

I catch her softly touching the glass with the tips of her fingers as the black fish swim around the other creatures inside like playful terriers. I wonder if she is perhaps reminiscing about the night she climbed into the chamber in an attempt to end her own mad genius. It occurs to me that she might have known the severance effect the foetal fluids would have had on her and had intended the genius to be wrenched from her and transformed into some beautiful, dangerous creature that could be contained or killed.

But instead it had been a much darker, uglier part—the door to the vault that locked her humanity inside and enabled her alienation, or perhaps her alienation itself—that had been warped and left to climb out. A part, regardless of what it was or where it came from, that she could not live without.

And so I continue with my part in the project which spawned me and each night I await the Project Leader to come to me and wrap her arms around me. l let her do so for I know that she needs me, this severed part of her—even though I feel nothing in return.

the

method

of

pulse

the method of pulse

Towards the end of time, in the middle of a vast mechanical wasteland, there are two points of existence.

He is the first.

His body is emaciated and ragged; he wears his own skin like the ill-fitting boiler suit that he is clothed in. He is a faded, lonely figure, dragging himself through the rubble of broken pneumatics and television screens that hiss static as if it were the word of some electronic god. His worker's boots are worn through the steel plating in their lining, the elbow and knee pads on his suit plagued by holes and tears. A pair of welding goggles hang from his neck, reflecting the distant swelling of the city from which he has escaped to come find her.

And she, she is the second point of existence.

She is a pulse in a jar—a heartbeat trapped in a plexi-glass chamber, diluted within the crystalline water that preserves the final piece of her. She has been reduced to this by the experimentation of the research project she found herself a part of whose purpose, it seemed to her, was to reduce her to the very focal point of her life; to re-tract the wasteful extremities of body and soul and see what was left.

And so she is a walnut-sized circle of blue light floating in a jar perched atop an empty toxic waste drum. She is il-luminated from one side by the glare of a TV screen as she throbs rhythmically. She is utterly vulnerable to the great black creatures that glide through the smoke-filled sky, amidst the tattered transmission waves of dead broadcasting stations. The networks no longer need an audience for their message has been fully assimilated.

The ground beneath his feet is like black mallow in places and so he climbs from piece of debris to piece of debris; across and along great wide girders, beneath the crumbling archways of buildings long gone, using hub caps and speaker drums as stepping stones and steadying himself occasionally on the rib-like iron rods exposed by cracked concrete walls.

It is quiet out there, save for the degenerative hiss of broadcast static. He is glad of that, if nothing else.

He cannot remember his part in the project—which pieces of her he removed or how. He imagines that perhaps he was never told what he was doing, just that he was to do it. His part in the production line was as fixed as everyone else's and just as isolated. There was no knowledge beyond that which was necessary to complete his task. They had each played an equivalent part in her deconstruction, each no more responsible than the last, and yet he still felt it was all his doing.

It was a week since the project had completed their work on her and with each day that had passed, nestled neatly between the steady heartbeat of his repetitive, unending task like a piece of rogue programming code, his thoughts of her had spawned. Her destruction had become as a virus re-writing him, breaking down his routine and leaving the ones and zeros of his binary existence to fall to the factory floor as she once had.

His re-mixed self, version 2.0, had climbed out of the research facility that previous night, pulled itself over the high barbed-wire fencing and then through cobbled streets ruptured in places by burgeoning fuel pipelines. His boots struck heavy upon the ground as he had passed the hi-rises at the edge of the city and then entered the wasteland that lay outside, where the machines were left to die. Hundred-foot high pylons stand wretchedly against the skyline like great broken scarecrows.

And what had remained as he had made the journey was a question—could he complete the **undo** command?

Could he complete *her*?

A few hundred yards ahead, beyond great broken coils and a car engine, he watches her. He had known that this was where she would be for this was where all wreckage was brought, where he too would be brought one day soon once he had become obsolete.

And yet, so close to her, he has stopped.

He sees the glistening heads of nailbombs studding the ground around her. Of course the facility wouldn't just leave her out there. She was garbage but she was *their* garbage—their in-built consumerism wouldn't let them give up ownership even after they had finished with her.

The devices are scattered around her, buried at varying depths and he assumes many are underground just enough to conceal the trigger mechanism but not to stop it working should he step on it.

He glances down at a CCTV monitor half-embedded in the ground beside him as if it were another bomb just waiting to fill his mind with jagged shards of MTV. In its static he sees himself broken down into thin ribbons and strips of bone as nails and chunks of aluminium tear through him and the Mekkanikal God has spoken—redemption through self-sacrifice.

She continues her beautiful rhythm as the sky crackles above them, so full of electricity that it glows at its edges.

And he takes his first step into the minefield.

The earth is sludge beneath him but so full of debris and semi-buried machine parts that it is near-solid. He seeks out the nearest visible bomb, breathes once—then steps on it.

In cinema-like perfection the trigger mechanism kicks the main device three and a half feet into the air where it hangs menacingly for a single moment, as if to fully relish its task, and then explodes in a sudden flash of fire and phosphorous light. A thousand tiny projectiles tear into him and through him and as he falls to the ground he leaves an arm behind, which drops a second later as if unable to comprehend gravity now that it has to think for itself.

He shudders on the ground momentarily before getting to his feet. His body leans to one side, unevenly weighted now, and he has to steady himself against a wedge of concrete.

Lightning strobes through the clouds and he sees her jar is lying on one side, its lid broken in two and the liquid that held her spilling out onto the mud below. She remains a pulse - but is now held tenderly in the palm of a thin, blue-veined arm whose shoulder joint trails off into the darkness.

Around him, radios scan excitedly from empty station to empty station, the thrum of dead air like locust swarms swooping close to him then fluttering away. Discarded strip-lighting glows softly and LCD displays give out meaningless rows of numbers.

He takes another step towards her, towards the completion of her, and another nailbomb sails insect-like into the air beside him before caressing him with a multi-faceted kiss. His right boot is shredded, pieces of its metal underside sinking into his foot and he falls once more, falls into the ground and sets off another bomb.

A TV set explodes nearby in exaltation.

The sky is humming.

And she is growing, pieces of her climbing out of the static air and completing her bit by bit.

He feels no pain, even as he is reduced to a torso by another, smaller bomb set into the impact zone of a bigger one and thus triggered a moment behind the first. He simply rewrites his own code—exchanges a one for a zero in his pain-receptor routine. He can make his own suffering obsolete by the mere flick of a binary switch.

He crawls towards her on one arm. The aerials poking out of the cacophony of devices that have come to watch swivel maniacally like the twitching of a rainforest beetle.

He is taken apart a little more.

As her re-assembly continues she slumps over the toxic waste drum, a jolt running through her body with each new piece that is added. She has become the ultimate consumer, wasting nothing in her re-acquirement of the flesh. The pulse that she once was is now hidden deep inside her chest cavity, throbbing quietly.

Now robbed of any self-mobility the remaining explosions take it upon themselves to carry him forward, dropping the unnecessary parts as they go, flipping him forward as he is reduced further and further.

Lighting flashes high overhead, feeding directly into the electricity pylons that lead the way to a digital heaven.

The drum suddenly bursts under the new weight and she falls into a spillage of semi-congealed engine oil threaded with glowing veins as if it were embryonic fluid birthing her. She writhes slowly, again as a new-born would.

The ground ignites beneath what is left of him, sparks and jets of pale fire illuminating the darkness, shattering television screens and computer monitors. He has been reduced to near-zero, a hexadecimal non-existence. He rolls towards her, the final fragments falling away and as he comes to a halt he is nothing but a walnut-sized piece of blue light.

His final reduction; his core.

His redemption fulfilled.

She rises from the mechanical fluids anew, glistening beneath her oily coating, her eyes and teeth pure white, her mouth of the deepest red.

The sky has gone quiet, the static roar of the broadcasts fallen to a background hush.

She looks upon the wasteland around her and then kneels. She picks up the jar that has fallen to the sodden ground and places it next to him, the strange little alien creature that he has become. Nudges him into it.

She hears his comfort in the steady beat of his pulse; his sadness.

She picks up the jar's lid and fixes it on.

"Safe now," she whispers.

A streak of static lightning sears the black, smog-filled sky and there is a low, broad rumble that is felt more than heard. White noise fills the TV screens. A scrolling LED banner spews out an endless line of binary code that quickly becomes zero after zero after zero.

She considers the towering skyline of the city behind her as distant memories of what came before this new version of herself emerge.

Then she turns, into the vast, unending plains of debris and dead air, with her lover in her hands and in her head. And, with the jar nestled in the crook of one arm, she walks towards the skyline, where Heaven meets Earth, where the production line has come to a confused halt and where the static is nothing but a comforting, if somewhat jagged, lullaby.

iron lung

Her hair is lank and hangs from her like knotted rope. It is of the blackest black. Her thin face is a sculpture of sharp features, her eyes feline green gashes amidst dark-smudges of sorrow.

I watch her through the curved window set into the iron lung I have put her in as she sleeps and imagine being in there with her as if we were two ghouls intertwined in a coffin fit for Poe's fetid imagination. That is my dream, to be in there with her, but I cannot climb inside. I must watch over her, protect her.

In a few hours she will be screaming and clawing once more at her pneumatic prison but for now she is as peaceful as depression itself. The great steel rods that breathe for her slide in rhythmical patterns all around the massive contraption, hissing at me and spewing hot greasy steam at odd angles. Rusted cogs turn in aged circles, grinding against one another, sparking. Differently coloured fluids pulse through thin copper veins.

I kiss the glass before her lips and whisper a prayer of solitude to her as she stirs ever so slightly on her ice-white pillows.

In this place I built for us there are now three rooms, each no bigger than six paces in any direction. It's not good for a person to have any more than that space around them at any one time which was why I had already sealed off two of the other annexes that I had initially built. In a world as big as the one above our haven there's too much room for dangerous creatures. So we have to break it down, make it smaller—and the smaller the better.

We all began life in a 1½ foot cocoon and Nature chose to put us there. She knows that we need protected just as I am protecting Lydia and myself from The Horrors Above. We were not meant to be broadening horizons, exploring or expanding the world around us. We should be shutting it down, building cages to put ourselves in, breaking the vast expanse of the dark skies and glowing endless deserts into manageable fragments, like pieces of a lunatic's psychosis.

I have come to the smallest of all the rooms, just big enough for me to slide inside. I curl within, my back matching the contours of the hole perfectly so that not even the smallest of predators can creep up on me.

The walls of this place are a mix of hard rock, tinted orange from the iron ore that laces them, and soft, crawling dirt. I have fitted steel girders along the rock, bolted them in place to stop anything breaking through. I try not to think about the potential millions of itching, scavenging, squirming creatures that I know are mere inches from us at any one time but I can hear them so clearly that it often becomes impossible. I listen to their chitinous scrapings, the rustling of their twisted bodies as they pass through loose soil. I listed to the muffled squawks, growls and groans. I listen to their manifold heartbeat and it sickens me.

Far above them, however, are the ones whom we truly fear.

I know not how far under we are—only that it is not far enough to cease feeling the rumble of vehicles passing far overhead, or sense the workings of the pipes and electrical systems that feed them like the IV's I have plugged Lydia up to within the iron lung.

Sometimes I feel one of them stopping where they stand and looking down, through the cracks in the sidewalk, through the dark mud beneath and the layers of life that have gone before and now lie beneath their feet like discarded snakeskin—and straight at Lydia and I.

I fear for the day they finally reach us.

I awaken to the sweet, sweet sound of Lydia screaming from within the iron lung and rush through to her.

The window is steamed from her exertions and in that sheen are the first claw marks she will make this night. There will be more to come.

I place a hand on the contraption's metal, warmed from the constant machinations of its parts, and offer soothing words to her through the inch-thick skein. I see her eyes wide beyond the fog of her terror-breath and make sure she can see me through the window at all times so that she will know I am there, still watching over her, still protecting her. As I always will be.

The iron lung jerked beneath me as it struggled to keep up with Lydia's bodily systems kicking in so suddenly and so emphatically, to maintain the industrial symbiosis that kept her safe in there. Pistons fired on every side and I heard the splash of engine oil hitting the ground beneath it. Life fluids circled through the lung's translucent veins, glowing with the speed they travelled at and once more I was struck by how the device was the most perfect thing I had ever seen.

Lydia bucked around inside but there was very little room for her to manoeuvre and she was still bloody and sore from her last concerted effort to escape.

I wish I could explain to her how safe she was there and how peaceful she could become if she learned to accept the lung's gentle steel embrace. There hadn't been time before I had stolen her from The Horrors Above and brought her to our sanctuary and anything that might infect the purity of her shelter had to be avoided. It pained me, but I couldn't allow myself the time to open the lung even for the short time it would take to soothe her properly.

Instead I had to watch the fear that gripped her, and now the madness that I glimpsed beginning to creep into her bright eyes. It was not right that she should suffer in this way while I remained enlightened as to the necessity of our retreat.

And so, to show her that she need not suffer alone, I retrieved the small canister of dirty water that I had collected from an exposed pipe over the weeks and selected three stones from the pile that lay beneath the lung. I always chose the most jagged ones I could find and placed them one by one upon my tongue. Then, using the water as a lubricant, I swallowed each fragment.

They ground down my trachea like outraged animals, cutting the soft flesh of my throat and peeling away the soft lining so that the hot sting of my own blood joined the feast. My body shuddered at the unwelcome rubble but I forced them all down, coughing up blood and phlegm as I worked, and finally collapsing to the ground.

I could feel the pieces wedged inside my stomach, my intestine, trapped in my veins. They were a glorious sediment for they demonstrated my commitment to Lydia and my being as one. One would not suffer without the other. One would not feel joy or love without the other. One would not breathe without the other.

I struggled to my feet, the extra weight now inside me making it more difficult, and slumped onto the iron lung as it panted and rumbled beneath me.

Lydia had ceased thrashing around for now. The window had cleared and I watched her as she lay half-twisted into the pillows, grabbing fistfuls of them and crying into them. Small smears of her anaemic blood sprinkled her pale skin where she had injured herself.

I so wished I could touch her.

But this was for the best. As long as she was in there nothing could get to her.

I lay down at the base of the iron lung's struts—four concrete slabs that were heavily greased to prevent anything from crawling up them—and curled my arms around one of them. I imagined it to be Lydia's arm as I closed my eyes to the sound of her muffled cries.

As The One Who Hides sleeps they begin to move around him, just beyond the mesh that layered the inner walls. They have watched from within the dirt for so long now, aroused by the fear that seeps from him like a pheromone. Their eyes swivel in the darkness, leeching what little light there is. They have been sent by The Horrors Above, tiny black messengers to let him know that he will not escape him. He is never safe from them.

The first wave are those with great gnawing teeth and bladed claws that bite through the steel mesh and peel it away to make way for the second and third waves—those of the many legs and feather-walks, the skittering, flooding, writhing movements.

They drip from the ceiling and squeeze themselves from the surrounding rock in total, oblique silence as they move towards the great device. They swarm across it and a single, fat grub-like creature presses its gluey body against the glass window as they begin to work their way inside.

My eyes fluttered open to a sound like the whisper of desert wind through a shattered cow skull. I rolled onto one side, the stones within me rattling against each other, colliding with my bones.

Everything was still, captured by the oil lamp that burned as long as I fed it from the iron lung's spillages. But I could sense the predators, the lurking hatred, the eyes that always watched us.

Why wouldn't they leave us alone?

The pneumatic wheeze of the lung's workings soothed my heartbeat as I stood, intently watching the tiny shadows all around me. I dared one of them to show themselves. Reaching for the toolbelt that I kept around my waist I took from it a claw hammer flaked orange with rust and raised it defiantly.

I had another roll of steel mesh tucked away behind one of the girders and had decided to layer it over that which I had already pinned to the stone walls. I had also begun to consider sealing off the second annex. The more rooms there were, the more places for them to break through.

Like a gentle breathing, the iron lung hissed at me and I smiled as I touched its cold skin. But the smile fell away as I noticed a translucent jelly smearing the window and the empty, bloodied pillows within the device.

And so my shock and fear were as numb and sharp and merciless as the steel bolt that Lydia drove through my shoulder as she stood behind me.

My body spat hot, hot blood and as I fell I glimpsed the hulking black shapes spilling out of the walls around me and poor Lydia's wretched form looming over me, her emaciated body torn and bleeding and staring madly down at me.

The iron lung hummed warmly around me, the encrusted pillows crackling beneath my every movement, flaking Lydia's blood like tiny feathers. My breath steams in the window but quickly clears.

She is watching me calmly from the other side, pieces of her scalp showing through where she has pulled the hair out. Her deep green eyes seem to have vanished into the back of her head leaving pits of empty blackness in their place. Her lips are swollen and cracked, her nose ringed with dried blood. She is mouthing hateful words that I find myself struggling to comprehend over and over again but which I don't need to. Her malice is clear in her very gait and I wish she could understand what she has done.

They will be coming for her. They may have given her freedom but now the deal was finished they would be coming for her.

And I scream into the stinking, airless container she has put me in because I know that they are in here with me, in the iron lung's veins, it its cracks and imperfections and soon they will be finding their way into mine. I cannot move my arms nor legs—there is no room. I can barely breathe. The stones weigh heavy in my bloodied chest.

They are in here with me.

And Lydia and I will never be truly safe.

akin to insects

Sitting in the corner of the club, I wondered if any of the others from the Electric Diva Initiative were tracking the same prey as me. On that first night they had let me join their little group I had instantly recognised several of them, though at first I couldn't recall exactly where from—there had been so many clubs, alleyways, temples and backstage wonderlands that they all kind of blurred after a while.

Just like the deities that drew me there in the first place.

I had been obsessing about ReDMeTaL for a few weeks now; my warm-up period. I'd attended every one of his performances, learned where he lived, what he did when he wasn't performing, his background (what little there was of it), his sexual preferences. For the past few nights, to mark my ever-nearing closeness to him, I'd etched his name onto my chest just above my breasts with a knife.

Other names at various points of fading away littered my skin.

The club was a converted bunker that consisted of four rooms and four corridors and I imagined that if you could stare down on the building from above it would form something pretty close to a swastika. There was no stage when ReDMeTaL was performing. He was hidden somewhere nearby, hooked up to all his equipment, pumping out the music that filtered through the club and kept everyone moving like liquid corpses as if it were his very blood itself that flowed.

I could see the hoards of other groupies (not pro's like me, just part-time obsessionals) mixed in with the genuine fans; the people who really did care about ReDMeTaL and his music and weren't just along for a ride with the hottest new thing.

"Isn't it wonderful?" someone who had seated themselves next to me asked. "Isn't he a genius?"

The someone was a boy, a young boy that somewhat resembled a length of wire that had been bent and twisted by a talented hand to form a human shape. His lizard-eyes had fallen back into his head thanks to one too many stokes on the communal bongs that were doing the rounds.

I drew on my cigarette, preferring to maintain my lucidity as I blackened my lungs, and let the smoke drift into the strobing, multi-coloured air.

"I've been to every one of his gigs," the boy continued.

Competition?

"Do you think he'll put in an appearance this time? I've heard he sometimes puts on some pre-recorded shit and walks into the venue to watch everyone listen. He could be here right now! He could be me! He could be y—Well, he couldn't be you, obviously. But he could be *that* guy."

He nodded towards a towering figure that looked like a great black waterfall—thick strands of jet black hair, a long heavy leather coat, a constant stoop, a pre-Mechanical Animals Marilyn Manson draped in latex. I drew on my cigarette, biding my time.

You couldn't rush these things. I still wasn't sure how I felt about this one. A groupie like me had to constantly calculate the equation of effort to value to determine whether it was all worth my time. If you took too long and the prey had already whored themselves too many times then it was really no conquest and no one gave a shit. On the other hand, if you struck too early, before they were worth anything, then there was no point. You'd be fucking a nobody and that was just a plain waste of time and bodily fluids.

"We used to be into Gristleback," another voice said and I hadn't even noticed the pixy-blonde creature lurking beside the boy. She wore a tight red dress that had been adorned with metal rivets with a distinct home-made quality about it. "It's almost embarrassing to say that now. What ever happened to them?"

"Who gives a shit?" the boy said and the two began dope-giggling.

I didn't mention the beautiful lower back muscles that I remembered Algieri, Gristleback's vocals and lead guitar, had. The way they moved like a family of finely-carved slugs beneath his skin as we 69'ed. How his semen tasted of absolutely nothing at all.

The strobing stopped in time with the music, which had fallen into a low industrial drone that could have been sampled straight from Lynch's original 110-minute version of *Eraserhead*. The u-v lighting took over, strips of glowing white reducing everyone to those parts of themselves that could reflect it. Suddenly the club was full of wandering torsos and boots, strange floating hairdos and metal panelling. I looked down at my arms and smiled as my scars glowed back at me as if they were fissures looking into Heaven.

I had been at enough ReDMeTaL gigs by now to recognise the end of a set and knew that drone was the start of it. The end of a gig was always the worst time to catch the performer because that was when they expected the fans to converge. I don't know what I'd been waiting for that night but I'd missed my chance.

No problem though—there were plenty of other gods to obsess about and the night was still young.

"We're akin to insects," Marina told me one night not long after I'd joined her little group. "We swarm on fresh corpses and take what we can before it's all gone. Then we move to the next corpse; and the next".

"And when there are no corpses?" I asked.

Marina smiled. "There are *always* corpses, little one."

She called all of us little one though she was barely three years older than me, like she considered us all her children.

It was early morning and everyone had returned to the mill from their nightly excursions. The jar that sat on a bench in the middle of the room was half-full of several inches of thick, pearly substances that swirled and danced with one another. I watched how they glittered in the low lighting.

The mill had been abandoned by the steel workers that had once used it long ago and for some reason it had been chosen as our resting place. Great, dirty windows looked out onto the parched wasteland that lay around us and the outskirts of the city of Seattle beyond. The walls were high and charred from decades of black smoke and smelt-air, their crumbling surfaces criss-crossed by support girders like a rusted exo-skeleton. The place had four levels but we mostly only used the first floor—an open plan work area that had been cleared of all the machinery that could be moved and left mostly unfurnished. It had, however, been decorated with delicately embroidered duvets that we lay on and strips of sarong material that draped the walls and reminded me of a Turkish whore house. Fist-sized golden foil stars had been pasted to the brick-work, glitter covered everything. We had done our best to make this our fairy-princess palace

Marina encouraged us to preen each other, to make our-selves even more beautiful, as we related our tales from that night.

I lay in her lap side-on, my head rested in the crook of her arm as she combed my hair with a diamond-studded hairbrush. We were all high on fairy-dust and many still buzzed from that night's activities. It was strange how empty you felt going back there without the smell of rut-ting on your skin or the taste of semen in your mouth.

"You must have a secret," Marina murmured, stroking my hair, "to have had so many in such a short space of time."

I hadn't lied when she had first come to me and de-manded I qualify myself for her little group. I had reeled off each conquest in chronological order having to skip back to retrace my steps every now and again. It was only when I'd mentioned Cobain's name that things had really snapped into place, a few of the others leaning closer, sceptical. In the end, I'd handed her a piece of skull. It could have been anyone's, I guess, but she took me at face value. She told me I'd only just beaten Courtney to it, from what she'd heard on the grapevine.

"So do you have a secret?"

I shrugged and the drugs made the movement feel earth-shattering. I felt like I would loose my balance and gripped Marina's shoulder. The air sparkled around us, full of PCP particles and the glitter that someone had thrown into the air conditioning units.

"I started young," I told her, and smiled. She met my eyes and smiled back.

A change of clothing, a change of approach.

I was on the west side the next night, having left earlier than usual. The others still slept on their prin-cess-blankets, coiled around one another like snakes. I was wearing the biggest, heaviest pair of hobnails the girls could find for me, a PVC mini and a latex crop-top covered by a light t-shirt patterned with a spiderweb design. I had streaked my hair with blue and green and red and put back in my lip and septum piercings.

My footsteps were meaner, heavier as I stalked the cobbled street. These were the parts of Seattle that had avoided all attempts at modernisation. This was where the Thurston Moore and Kurdt Cobain plagues left their dead and dying—in small, scabrous nightclubs and run-down venues, most of which didn't even have signs outside.

I walked past them all, past the rabbles that roamed around outside them, past the HIV-infected bouncers with their virus-bruised eyes, past the dealers and whores. Two nights earlier I had stalked Esther as she walked these very streets.

Esther was a gloriously tall, angular diva and from what I had gathered one of the first to have joined Marina. She didn't like me much, being that Marina paid so much attention to me now and I have a policy to dislike anyone who dislikes me. I knew she had been after the self-named mechanical guru DemiFlesh for almost as long as I had, maybe longer. I'd heard about him long before joining the Divas but had kind of put him on the back-burner when ReDMeTaL and a few others had come along. The guy made himself very difficult to find which was both a challenge I liked and good sign—when they made it so easy for you to get close to them they weren't worth getting close to in the first place. And I admit that, for me, it's always been a case of quantity not quality. Well, fuck, it got me into the Sisterhood, didn't it?

But now times were a-changing. I wanted to show the others how dedicated I was to my obsessions and how good I was at what I do.

I'd fallen behind in the times, however, and had no idea where DemiFlesh was at now. It was only after overhearing Esther discuss the man with another diva the week before that I'd gotten the break I needed. She'd worked her stuff enough to get a personal meeting with him in one of his machine-temples and for us girls there was only one thing that meant.

I stood by the subway entrance I had followed Esther to previously. It led to a part of the underground that hadn't been in use for decades and there were strips of yellow crime scene tape and broken barriers across the entrance. The steps were worn and filthy.

Quietly, I descended.

The platform was covered in litter and lit with a grey light that emanated from an opening in a wall up ahead across the railtracks. Before, I had watched Esther climb through the hole, watched her sit with a dozen others on plastic mats that had been spread out on the floor of what was at one time a way-station for subways cops (the broken porcelain tiles and upturned lockers attested to it). The apostles had been bent forwards, facing a giant TV screen displaying nothing but raw static. Beneath it, a man was wrapped up in razorwire, his limbs outstretched and plugged into fat coils of tubing that in turn were connected to a makeshift machine that arced over his head. His eyes had glowed with the electricity that flowed through him. Flickering images from his head had flashed across the screen as his followers had murmured their worship.

I leapt from the platform onto the dead tracks and went once more to the hole. I checked my watch and smiled—the drug I had slipped Esther would keep her under for another three or four hours by which time DemiFlesh would be mine and we would both be fucked, if in completely different ways.

I stepped through the opening. The room seemed empty apart from that giant TV screen churning out static. The plastic mats had been rolled into tubes and lay at the edge of the room. There was a doorway to my left that I hadn't been able to see before, draped in strips of wafer-thin sheet metal like a curtain.

I peeled the curtain aside and there he was, strapped into what had to be an electric chair, his wrists and ankles shackled to the solid oak with thick black cuffs. There were wires sticking out of him that glowed red and blue where they curved and all around were miniature TV screens, the pre-pubescent minions of the monster in the first room. The walls were constructed entirely of these screens, packed tight against one another like bricks. Some were dead or broken; most sparkled with static.

"You're not Esther," DemiFlesh said. Or, to be more precise, the TV screens said.

I slinked towards him, not even having to think about becoming the reptilian, all-in-the-hips creature I needed to be. My boots made noisy contact with the concrete floor.

At that point, I was pretty sure he was the real thing. I had been wrong in the past, falling for the charms of self-professed mekanikal messiahs like Dario or Reubens-The-One-Who-Will like some sort of hormonal blonde, but there was something about the energies in the room with us . . .

It was like God himself had been broken down in particles of black, grey and white and floated in those screens.

"I'm not Esther," I agreed, standing before him.

Then I knelt between his opened legs, brushed aside my hair and did what I do best.

I'm not quite sure of the protocol of what I did with DemiFlesh—stealing him from Esther like that. Nobody ever explained any rules involved in the Electric Diva Initiative but I guess some things shouldn't have to be said. Winning a fuck from another groupie is one thing but drugging them and stealing it from under their noses is quite another.

But fuck, every girl for herself, right?

It somehow turned out to be a much longer walk back than I had figured and I reached the palace a little after three while most of the girls were still out. There were maybe five lounging around the prettily-decorated machines, including a Chinese girl named Anna and, of course, Esther—still out for the count beneath her purple and gold duvet.

My jaw was aching from holding the little gift I held in it so I hurried to the jar. Anna moved towards me and watched me spit the semen into the container, still to be filled by the others. Anna handed me a facecloth and I wiped my chin.

She was a typically Orientally-delicate creature with bone structure most of us would kill for. Her eyes were more rounded than you'd expect, hitting that babydoll look like a marksman and she never wore anything that went beyond mid-thigh. But she'd made a mistake a month or so back and was now full of a virus that seemed to be gutting her like a fish. She bled constantly, having to wad herself with small towels that needed changed every few hours. Her skin had faded three shades since I'd met her and she hadn't been out for a week now.

"You left early tonight," she said in that bamboo-hard voice.

"I had an appointment."

"Tell me?"

I wasn't really in the mood but there was a desperation in the girl's voice that touched me. She hadn't been able to starfuck for how long now? I couldn't imagine not being able to do this –it would drive me insane.

So we settled against an industrial oven that had once turned steel to a hot, red oil, padding our backs with cushions as I wrapped her in my arms. I told her about DemiFlesh—she'd heard of him but only vaguely—embellishing the story as I saw fit and of course missing out certain duplicitous parts.

"I think Esther was after him too," Anna whispered, drifting off slightly.

"Doesn't look like she was putting much effort into it," I replied and we both looked towards the woman, sprawled out on the floor snoring loudly. How unladylike.

I told Anna how he sparked when I touched him and how I saw images from my childhood in the TV screens and how when he came it felt like it was metal shavings that poured into my waiting mouth.

"Was he for real?" she asked me as she lingered at the edge of sleep.

I nodded, running my finger across her brow. "Pretty sure."

"Are you going to tell Marina?"

"Of course."

But by the time I'd answered, Anna was already asleep.

Kill your gods.

To destroy what matters most is to destroy everything in one fell swoop. To destroy a fraud is to waste time and energy.

In a world as desolate as this one, there is an unbound freedom for mechanical deities to rise from the ground and fall into the waiting sky. And there is an unbound freedom for those who are not gods to become followers of gods—for those are the only two choices.

Find your god—then consume it.

There were twelve of us, roosting in the crumbling framework that roofed the top of the subway tunnel like great, decorated bats. We had gathered in the daylight above, descended into the tunnel then waited.

Esther was noticeably absent—either still out of it or sulking. Maybe it was just jealously not only that I had gotten to DemiFlesh first but that he seemed to be the real thing. Or maybe she knew (at least suspected) how I had managed it. Her hands were tied, of course—there was nothing she could do.

I looked across to Anna, who had begged to come along. She was wrapped around a rafter, coated in a gold and purple smock and large shining earrings, staring right at me.

I stared right back.

We fell silent at the sound of the movement from the dark recesses at the end of the tunnel. A flickering light followed it, glances of silver in the blackness as what little illumination there was hit the pieces of aluminium that DemiFlesh adorned himself with to enable better conductivity. A buzz seemed to follow him—electrons like flies swarming around him.

I looked across to Marina—we all did—and she had that same look in her eye as she did when I had told her about DemiFlesh earlier that night; when she had dipped a finger into the jar and tasted the dead semen of a god. Her eyes were partially closed, the tiara she wore tilted on her puffed-up hairdo, her lips swollen with freshly self-injected collagen.

Like Betty Boo with a serial killer's psychosis.

DemiFlesh drew nearer, travelling along the train tracks, almost hovering. A handful of large, thick-tailed rats scurried after him, attracted by the charge he gave off. In the shadows, the girls and I could see things sparking off of him; images and memories and futures, as if he were a psychic hard drive spilling its contents.

Marina nodded solemnly. He was the real thing.

We waited until he was under us, just about to climb though the hole into his lair, then drew our weapons.

We dropped onto him in a blinding flash of lipstick, nail varnish and stiletto blades and began the rape and murder of this new-found deity.

Sometime later we were all sprawled out on the train tracks, bloody and tired and exhilarated as we swam in the afterglow. Our outfits were torn, ruined, our heads buzzing with whatever powers had filled DemiFlesh before we had broken him open.

Better than sex.

I rolled onto one side, listening to the soft, exhausted laughter of the others. We lay curled in each other's laps, the nape of each other's backs, spooned into one another. Around the sallow-white curve of little Elizabeth's shoulder, I watched Marina.

She lay draped backwards across a barrier which ran along the middle of the tunnel wall, either something to protect the trains from colliding with the stonework or something to assist anyone unlucky enough to have fallen into the pit where the tracks lay. The long purple dress she had worn was split almost entirely up one side, and I studied the figure beneath. A drop of blood formed like a tear in a wound on her thigh, spilled out. Her hair, crimped into tight, glossy curls, hung parallel to her long legs. There was a wide smile on her face.

She turned abruptly from staring at the ceiling to me and I didn't have time to look away. She'd caught me looking at her a number of times before and fixed me with that same curious, angelic expression.

She blew me a kiss with blood-smeared fingers.

I caught it with a dirty hand and pressed it to my heart as I lay back down.

When we arrived home Esther was waiting for us, perched on an oil-drum that had been spray-painted with gold shimmer paint and wearing a smile so wide it had to be drug-assisted. Her mescaline-filtered attention was drawn into focus as we spilled into the palace and she somehow managed to find me amongst the crowd.

She landed me with her fat-cat grin, unwrapping her elegant calves from one another as she stepped down from the drum. She swept flakes of rust from her buttocks, her head tilted to one side. Sweet, fucking angelic.

The others had gone to where they were going—the rafters, the staircase, bunks, mattresses, the tubs—chattering excitedly, high on orgasm and more. I felt Marina come up behind me, her arm sliding around my waist, fingers spreading against the lower half of my stomach and we both looked at the woman.

"Esther?" Marina said, reproachful like a mother.

Esther placed a finger in her mouth and played the counterpart mischeavous child. Giggled. "Mommy's home."

Marina left my side but I followed her one step behind, not wanting to be away from the warmth of her body. I watched as she reached out and took something with the side of her finger from Esther's chin—a thin streak of milky liquid, no need to explain.

"You've been out tonight, little one?"

Esther nodded. "Uh huh." Then her eyes flashed on me and I was feeling all the excitement of that night draining from me, leaving me cold. "Had myself a *good* time."

Her eyes were full of sparks, fireworks based on the polymer-hybrid chains that she had obviously been consuming all night. She swayed before us, laying one hand on the drum to steady herself. A few of the other girls were watching us, their curiosity now aroused.

When Esther put her finger in her mouth again she smeared something over her face, something dark. When she noticed it, she glanced back at the drum and began to giggle.

Marina pushed past her and pulled at the lid of the drum, somehow managing to jerk it open without damaging her two-inch nails. I only had a chance to glance in before it was slammed back down again but it was enough for me.

How she had managed to squeeze him in there, I'll never know.

Who it *wasn't* in there, folded in half with a foot of steel wire wrapped around the base of his dick to enable Esther to suck him off even as he died of his injuries was clear right from the start, at least to me.

It *wasn't* ReDMeTaL liked Esther had hoped.

Who is *was* took me a few seconds longer—the kid from the club the week before. The one who had challenged that he could be ReDMeTaL, for all I know. Perhaps he had challenged Esther in a similar way or perhaps he hadn't even needed to go that far, depending on how hallucinogenic she was. Whatever, she had fallen for his wishful deception.

Some of the others had gotten rid of the barrel, tipping it into the nearby river after weighting it down with fresh cement. We girls were as talented with a nailgun and a blowtorch as we were with a nailfile and a blowjob. I had stayed with Marina as Esther had come down off her high—come crashing down.

Now she wouldn't stop crying or clawing at herself, screaming murder at her own veins as she tried to tear them open. I stood behind Marina, my arms wrapped around her and gently placed upon her mons, feeling nothing but utter satisfaction.

The whore had either tricked to what I was up to earlier or had known as soon as she figured she had been drugged and had reacted in the only way us super-bitches knew.

Cold, clean revenge.

"Please! PLEASE! God, Please!!" Esther screamed at us, at her self, at no one in particular. She wrapped herself in circles, kicking at fresh air, slamming her head into the concrete in anger and frustration.

She knew that she had failed, that she was out. We all did.

I stood there, watching as she beat herself towards death, my arms around Marina, my mother, my sister, gently fondling her in time with the pulse of blood leaking from Esther's bruised arms.

I couldn't have wished for a better night.

After Esther's "death", I somehow became elevated amongst our ranks, her failure somehow becoming my success. This led to a certain amount of complacency on my part and certainly the fairy dust and mescaline cocktails I took day and night could only have contributed to my uncommonly satiated drive for a good fuck. I let the others pamper me, I pampered myself. I still went out but aimlessly.

I didn't even try looking for a new idol.

Because even through my drug-haze, when Marina had whispered what she whispered in my ear one night soon after it had brought everything crashing down around me and it had also crushed everything into a solid, discernible shape. I had rolled onto my side as she repeated herself, just to see her lips make the movement.

Our secret, she had said. This is our secret.

I had smiled because all I could see was a future and it was star-bright with the one true god, the one that was Marina and I's secret. One that went far beyond ReDMeTaL, beyond Darius-X, beyond DemiFlesh and, yes, beyond Cobain himself. One whose orgasm would rip the top of my skull off as I brought them to and through it.

After a week and a half the fairy dust settled in my system like real dust resting on our makeshift furniture. Like real dust, like our skin, mixing in the air, flaking off, little dead pieces of human beings just like the ones buried in the riverbed somewhere nearby. What followed was a clarity made even more pure by the fog that had preceded it.

I smiled inwardly as I lay on my mattress, staring at the high industrial ceiling untouched by out meagre attempts at decoration. This starfuck would be the ultimate. I began to burn inside, feeling nothing but the desire to fuck and be fucked.

I was perched on the throne that I had had some of the girls build for me. We had stumbled across a bona-fide electric chair one night and had spent some time marvelling over the device—its charred wood, infused with the flesh of criminals, its rusted metal plating—where it lay in the state refuse dump. Then we had carried it all the way back to the palace for it was only right that a palace should have a throne. The only problem was, we had so many princesses that wished to perch their finely sculpted asses on it.

We had bolted sheets of brightly reflective aluminium stars to its dreary sides, sparkled a glitter and PCP mix on its old gnarled wood, fixed slashes of Middle-Eastern fabric along its breadth. We had built a platform on which the throne would stand but only after a while and so we had also had to build a pulley system by which to raise it up.

To begin with the girls had been as excited as I was but as it dragged on they grew bored, itchy for an orgasm that wasn't self-induced. And who could blame them? It was like butchers being told to paint walls—soon they were aching for a lump of red flesh to slice in two. It had been a distraction, of course.

My plan was formulating, the time bomb was ticking fast like a dance club rhythm, my anxiety and paranoia swelled and deflated as if it was a great ocean. It doesn't matter, I would tell them. We don't need another fuck just yet. How can we enjoy them if we can't savour them? And how can we savour them if we don't chew properly, or swallow patiently?

Trust me, I know. I have seen. In the meantime, we need to prepare.

As I watched them work, the bags that they hefted around spilling over with tins of grease and used amphetamine needles, with lipstick barrels and 3-inch clips for the nailguns, their beautiful muscles likes scurrying creatures, hard and eager, beneath their skin. So pretty amongst the dirt and the rust. Solid angels emerging from clouds of cement dust because I always wanted more, more for this creation that would be the centre of our worship.

And who should be placed upon it?

Tensions grew rapidly and I was all too aware. The girls resented me crapping on their excitement about a new idol, telling them not to waste their saliva because it was soon, soon and they did what I said even if they didn't like it because of my closeness to Marina.

Towards the end of the throne's creation they had been so crabby that I had had to finish it myself, adding the last finishing touch—a piece of driftwood hammered across the head of the chair horizontally to form a small cross against its straight back. I padded the seat with gold and purple cushions and stapled a length of shiny silver fabric to its frame to cover up the hollow underside.

Marina watched me from the back of the room, growing suspicious. She saw me talk to the others, saw how I could control them because they were so ready to *be* controlled—just as she had. She still lay next to me at night, still let me stroke her, but I think she might have begun to regret telling me her secret that night. We were together and apart; my mind was on her but also on the starfuck she had promised me. The one that would blow my mind. Blow both our minds.

Blow all our minds.

Was it the president? the girls asked.

Was it Elvis Presley, alive and well and living in Utah with enough semen to fill us all?

No, I told them as they lay gathered around me at the base of the throne, my legs tucked up on its huge seat, the iron band where the cap had once been hovering over me like a halo.

Was it Che Guevara's perfectly-preserved corpse; or Lenin's?

And their resentment almost overnight turned to excitement as I took on the role of storyteller, teasing them with Marina's promise.

No, I told them. Bigger.

Was it the Anti-Christ, wrapped up in suit-and-tie as if he were straight out of a Brett Easton Ellis novel?

No, I told them. Bigger.

Bigger.

When I was eleven years old, I remember being in church with my parents. It was only a few months before the fire that had killed them both and I had been left, as usual, to wander the churchyard afterwards while they made small talk with the rest of the flock. I played with the daisies then saw the daughter of one of my father's friends going around the back of the church, away from the sun. I followed her and found her before a massive statue of a crucified Jesus, the modern world's first revolutionary, a god in his own right. This is what she told me. The first revolutionary. That's Jesus Christ, I told her and she had said, yes, I know. Do you know what I would do if I ever met Jesus Christ or God? she had asked me. No. If I should I ever meet god in person, she told me, I would truly like to suck his dick.

Was it Charlie Manson?

Was it Ray Kroc, creator of McDonald's?

Was it the CEO of Nike or Disney or Wal-Mart? Was it Marshall McLuhan's ghost? Was it Denis Rodman? What colour would god be? And on what channel would he be broadcast? Would he be digital or analogue?

Or it could be a *she*, Anna had said, and then the excitement had tripled.

No, I told them. No.

And all the time Marina stood in her dark, absent corner, the only thing giving away her presence being the smoke she spat out at irregular intervals.

If god was a number, how many digits?

And if you finally met him after all those years of trying what would you say, what would you do?

Me, I'd suck his dick.

And so it was, Marina had told me the final secret, the one that would mean an end to all this and I had seen that perhaps even before she did. She had unleashed the

Antichrist, the Final Beast, and it was wanting to be fucked as hard as possible.

I had told the girls to be ready, that it was soon and they had stitched and sewn and hammered and nailed themselves all kinds of beautiful costumes as I had watched Marina lying on her mattress, suddenly so far away from us but that was okay, she would return to the fold. She was tired. She had led for so long and now she needed a rest.

She had revealed her secret, revealed the one true god, and she was still reeling from it.

I watched her every breath as she slept, counting the time between inhalations and exhalations. One night I lifted her and placed her in her throne because she still refused it. When she had woken, with me lying curled at her feet, she had gotten up blearily and stumbled back onto her mattress.

It didn't matter.

I spooned her into my lap and whispered in her ear.

"It's okay, we'll all be okay," because eventually all children have to look after their parents. Unless they die in a fire, that is.

"I don't understand any of this," she replied.

"Shhh," I said, and kissed her hair. "It'll all be over soon."

And two nights later it nearly was, what with the girls dead all around me and Marina nailed to her throne, nailed to the cross, mouth bloody and open, ready to receive Jesus Christ's dick.

"It's time," I had told the girls and instantly they were gathering around me.

Marina had gone out, she was the only one who still did but a short time earlier she had contracted syphilis, a nasty batch of red crust that nestled on her upper lip, and so she had had little success. But she would be back soon and then we could begin.

I stood on the platform the throne sat upon and they came towards me like true disciples, all glitter and glamour and flashes of thigh and hip and breast; lipstick smears, kohl stains like bruises and cheekbones heightened by the amateur cosmetic surgeons amongst us. In their handbags, make-up kits and rape alarms.

I could smell their sexuality in the air, musty and thick and desperate.

One by one they came to me for a postage stamp of specially-formulated acid, tonguing them one by one like the Eucharist. One by one they moved away.

With three left, in walked Marina, swaying slightly, sodden from the downpour outside.

"What's going on?"

I gave the last trio their tabs. "We're ready to meet god," I told her.

Marina looked around, at the girls, at their eagerness.

"We're going to suck his fucking *dick*," somebody cried, a chemically-unbalanced edge to their voice. Some laughter, some squealing.

Marina all sad and morose.

"This isn't right," she said. "What have you been telling them?"

"I used to go to church," I told her. "I used to be a virgin".

"Little one, what's been going on?" She said this, having walked towards me and now only a few feet away with her eyes full of liquid.

"I used to go to church," I told her again.

"I heard you. I went to church too. Honey, what's the matter?"

"I know you went to church too. I know which church you went to".

"C'mon are we going or not?" one of the girls whined. She was sweating from the rush of natural drugs soaring through her system. A moment later another collapsed, began to sieze.

Marina looked at the jerker, then at me, as the girls began to stagger. "What have you given them?"

Gina, a voluptuous ex-stripper and sometime car mechanic crashed into the concrete face first and I swear you could almost see the cartoon stars spilling out of the crack that was made.

" . . . . feel sick . . . ."

"Enlightenment," I told her.

That night, the secret-giving night, the night that opened the floodgates.

Marina lay beside me, sober and wide awake. "I always felt empty," she said to the darkness, to the cold night air. "So empty."

I took her hand in mine.

"Warm," she said. "I feel warm instead of empty. When you hold me."

I was facing away from her, looking at the great dirty windows punched into the opposite wall. I listened to what she told me and I thought about all the things I might tell her. About the pictures I had taken of her. About the many months I had followed her for a time, long before I arrived at the doors of the Electric Diva Initiative. About all the fantasies I had had of her raping me, drugging me then raping me, killing me then raping me; of her kissing me like moonlight kisses a vast, black ocean.

"I love you," she had whispered into my hair. This had been her secret.

I had remained facing the wall for a long time after she had turned over and gone to sleep. I lingered on her words.

"I have something to tell you. It's a secret. No-one can know. It's our secret."

And then the three words, like sticks of dynamite strapped to mink, beauty and blood entwined, that had followed.

"Enlightenment," I had told her when she had asked me what I had given the girls. Enlightenment, and enough 90-proof hallucinogen to topple their meek senses and minds within the half-hour.

"Did you mean it?" I asked her as Sara and Joolz and Tish collapsed into each other. "What you said?"

Marina watched as her makeshift daughters fell to the concrete, like two-dozen bridesmaids in their wonderful new clothes, like skittles or acorns. She put her hands to her mouth as tears spilled out over the backs of her palms; as Terese went to her knees then crawled onto the ground and then shook when she got there; as fragile, bone-china Anna spat her own blood out in great gobs.

Then we were right next to each other and my hand was on Marina's hip. I took her hand away and raised it to my mouth, kissed it. "Your majesty," I said and curtseyed.

Marina's lips quivered and so I kissed them too, to steady them. I clasped her head, drew her to me and gradually her mouth opened to mine and I let warmth flow from me into her.

When I meet god . . .

All those years ago, half my current life-span really. She hadn't changed much from the vaguely-adolescent girl

that had so enraptured me, her partially-formed breasts
cleaved into the her white blouse by the shadow thrown
by the church.

When I meet god . . .

I undressed her and she undressed me as our beautiful
army fell around us, under the spell of carbon and phos-
phates and unknown polymers. We stepped out of our
bridal gowns and out of our jewellery and still she let me
kiss her and indeed kissed back and when our skin
touched as I led her to her throne it ignited the small flame
that had been burning inside me all these years.

"What would you do if you met god?" she had asked me,
before another year of church as she blossomed before my
very eyes and I struggled to keep up with her from a distance because after my parents had died I no longer really
went to church.

"Me, I'd suck his dick," I said to the tombstones after she
had been driven away. I said it to the statue too.

Years later, my queen had been throned and she lay back
as I straddled her on its wide seat and we kissed. I pulled a
lever on the side of the throne that I had rigged up and
three pounds of PCP, cocaine and crunched-up amphet-
amines drifted down upon us so that when we drew our
tongues across each other's skin they crackled with drugs.

When I meet god I'd suck his dick . . .

And there she sat, crowned by the rusted halo as I slid
between her legs.

The girls that remained alive, that had survived my le-
thal cocktail, watched us writhe against one another and
knew that what they were witnessing *was* bigger, like I had
said. Was this god? they would ask themselves. Am I seeing god, multi-armed and sweating and so fucking unbe-
lievably sexy and carnal? And they would then die with
that thought as their hearts freaked out on my cocktail.

"What have you given them?" I had been asked.

"Enlightment," had been my answer.

As Marina arched beneath me, had bucked, had pressed
herself against me through the glittering drug-stardust, I
gripped her wrists and spread them above her, felt tiny
quivers run through her belly, felt her legs wrap themselves around my head and it was apocalypse now, I
thought *if god came would it shake the world dead*, and
thrust Marina's hands onto the nails I had embedded at
each end of the vertical plank that made my cross as she

climaxed, as blood flew from her wrists and spasms wracked her pelvic floor muscles.

Crucified, my wonderful princess, left to shudder against the cold wood as orgasm continued to surge and wouldn't let her cry out at the fire in her arms, bucking against her pain and her pleasure then sinking into both.

I stepped back down off the platform to watch, my face smeared with her moisture. Did she recognise me now? Or had she always known?

What would I do if I met god?

It was what she taught me that day.

Never to bow down. Never to admire because there was only one almighty being that had control over you and it wore your clothes and fucked your lovers and shared your bowels. All gods are false gods because there is only one you and if you were to find one of these fakers then you should kill it because it is a liar—not the minnows, not the ones that can't even *pretend* but instead the dangerous ones, the ones that convince, the ones that almost make it.

So there was Marina, slumped in her throne, pinned to a cross as her beauty-queen disciples lay scattered around her like poisoned roaches, her question finally answered.

I began to gather up my things, feeling ecstatic and orgasmic if not a little disorientated. I dressed in an old boiler suit and high heels because that's what was there. I picked up a nailgun and then a nail. I wrapped electrical wire around my hair to keep it out of my face. I loaded the nailgun.

I put some essentials in a sports bag and didn't contemplate what I would do next because that was too huge a question.

For now, I climbed up onto the platform before Marina, her eyes wide and wet but calm. Blood bubbles popped on her full, collagen-happy lips. I raised the nailgun and lined it up with the point where her eyebrows met.

And I fired.

Because what would I do if I met god?

I'd suck his dick—then I'd kill him.

Printed in the United States
3643